BATTLE FOR CORON

Battle for Coron

Daniel Avery Bacon

Forward

To the countless dreamers who dare to leap through portals, both real and imagined; to the unwavering spirits who fight for what is right, even when the odds seem insurmountable; and to the quiet whispers of inspiration that guide us through the darkest forests and into the brightest lights. For those who find solace in the embrace of fantasy, who seek adventure in the unknown, and who believe that even the most ordinary individual can become extraordinary when faced with the extraordinary. It is dedicated to the belief that even a struggling writer, burdened by self-doubt and a blank page, can find within himself a reservoir of courage and creativity, capable of facing down the most formidable foes and shaping the destiny of a kingdom. This story is for you. Let this tale remind you that within each of us lies a potential hero, a capacity for extraordinary acts, and a boundless wellspring of inner resilience.

1

The Unexpected Journey

The chipped mug warmed Gerald's hands, the lukewarm tea doing little to soothe the icy grip of anxiety constricting his chest. Outside, the city hummed with a life he felt utterly detached from, a spectator watching a play he no longer understood. His cramped apartment, usually a sanctuary of sorts, felt like a suffocating cage. Every surface was littered with the detritus of his creative struggle: crumpled sheets of paper, half-finished chapters, discarded plot outlines – a graveyard of unrealized potential. The air hung heavy with the scent of stale coffee and the lingering ghost of inspiration, a phantom he'd been chasing for months.

His new book, a high fantasy epic he'd envisioned as his magnum opus, lay dormant on his laptop, a cruel testament to his crippling writer's block. The initial burst of enthusiasm, the vibrant world he'd meticulously crafted had dwindled to a flickering ember, threatening to extinguish completely. The pressure mounted; the deadline loomed like a dark cloud, its shadow stretching across every aspect of his life.

He'd tried everything. He'd retreated to his favorite coffee shop, hoping the bustling energy of the city would ignite his creativity, but the noise only amplified the silence within. He'd taken long walks through the park, seeking inspiration in the natural world, but the trees seemed to mock his barren imagination. He'd even attempted those ridiculous writer's block remedies he'd read about online – listening to classical music, meditating, even trying to write with his nondominant hand – all to no avail.

Self-doubt gnawed at him relentlessly. Was he simply not talented enough? Had he peaked too soon? Were his initial ideas fatally flawed? The weight of expectation, both self-imposed and external, pressed down on him, suffocating his creative spirit. His agent's encouraging words felt distant and hollow, mere echoes in the cavern of his despair. The whispers of failure grew louder, casting long shadows over his future. He imagined the disappointed faces of his family, the mocking whispers of his peers, the crushing weight of financial ruin.

His apartment, a reflection of his inner turmoil, was a mess. Books lay scattered on the floor, their pages dogeared and stained with tea and coffee. Empty takeout containers formed a precarious landscape on his desk, remnants of countless late nights fueled by caffeine and despair. Even the usually comforting glow of his laptop screen felt cold and

accusing. He stared at the blank document, the cursor blinking mockingly, a digital metronome marking the passage of time, each tick a reminder of his failure.

He'd poured his heart and soul into this book, envisioning a sweeping saga filled with breathtaking landscapes, compelling characters, and intricate magic systems. He'd spent months researching, outlining, and world building, pouring over maps and mythologies, immersing himself in the rich tapestry of fantasy lore. Now, all that meticulous planning seemed futile, a monumental waste of time and energy. The intricate world he'd built within his mind felt distant, unreachable, like a forgotten dream.

He ran a hand through his messy hair, the strands falling back into place with the weight of his despair. The deadline loomed, a monstrous beast breathing down his neck, demanding a sacrifice he felt incapable of offering. He considered abandoning the project altogether, but the thought sent a shiver of guilt down his spine. He couldn't just walk away. This wasn't just a book; it was a part of him, an extension of his soul. He had to find a way, a way out of this creative wilderness, a way to reignite the spark that had once burned so brightly.

He slumped back in his chair, the cheap foam groaning under his weight. He closed his eyes, trying to conjure up the world he had created, the vibrant tapestry of Coron, a kingdom he had poured so much life into. But instead of vivid images, all he felt was a void, an emptiness that mirrored the hollowness within him. He was lost, adrift in a sea of self-doubt, with no land in sight, no compass to guide him, no hope to cling to. He was trapped, and the walls of his own mind were closing in.

He picked up a worn copy of "The Lord of the Rings," the familiar weight of the book offering a fleeting sense of comfort. He opened it randomly, his eyes falling on a passage describing the vast and awe inspiring landscapes of Middle earth. A strange tingling sensation ran down his spine, a prickling of energy that felt both exhilarating and unnerving. He looked up, his gaze drawn to the window. The setting sun cast long, distorted shadows across his desk, creating an eerie atmosphere.

Then, he noticed it. A shimmering, almost imperceptible distortion in the air, a ripple in the fabric of reality itself. It hung suspended in the air, a ghostly portal pulsating with an otherworldly light.

Hesitantly, he approached the anomaly, drawn by an irresistible force he couldn't comprehend. His mind filled with curiosity, doubt battling fascination. He took a deep breath, feeling the air thicken around him, the room's normal temperature suddenly shifting. His heart beat a frantic rhythm against his ribs, and his mind raced. He had been trapped by his writer's block, by the constant struggle to make sense of his own story, his own life. But now, something far more extraordinary was presenting itself. The portal shimmered, beckoning him forward, and a decision that would change his life forever hung in the balance. The shimmering light of the portal pulsed, its captivating glow promising adventure, offering escape, a solution perhaps to the creative drought that had plagued him. A voice, barely a whisper, seemed to call to him, promising a solution to the torment that became his reality. Hesitantly, he extended a hand, the air tingling as his fingers brushed against the shifting light. The scent of pine and damp earth filled his senses, a sharp contrast to the stale air of his apartment. And then, with a surge of both terror and excitement, he stepped through.

The world exploded in a kaleidoscope of emeralds and sapphire. One moment, Gerald was standing in his cramped apartment, the scent of stale coffee clinging to the air, the next, he was enveloped by a symphony of scents – the rich, earthy aroma of damp soil, the crisp, clean fragrance of pine needles, and the sweet, almost intoxicating perfume of unfamiliar blossoms. Giant trees, their trunks thicker than any he'd ever seen, soared into the sky, their branches interwoven to form a dense, emerald canopy that filtered the sunlight into an ethereal, dappled light.

He stood in a clearing, the grass beneath his feet soft and yielding, a vibrant green unlike any he'd encountered in his mundane existence. Flowers of impossible colors iridescent blues, shimmering violets, and a fiery orange that seemed to pulse with inner light – bloomed in profusion, their petals unfurling in a silent, graceful dance. Butterflies with wings like stained glass fluttered around him, their delicate bodies a vibrant contrast to the deep green of the foliage. Strange, melodic chirps and whistles filled the air, a chorus of unseen creatures that both fascinated and slightly unnerved him.

The scale of the forest was overwhelming. The trees were immense, their bark textured with ancient carvings that seemed to shift and change as he looked at them. Luminous fungi, radiating a soft, pulsating glow, dotting the forest floor, casting an eerie, yet beautiful, light upon the scene. The air itself felt different, charged with a palpable energy that hummed beneath his skin, a subtle vibration that resonated with his very being. He felt alive, invigorated in a way he hadn't felt in years, the creative block that had choked his spirit dissolving like mist in the morning sun.

He took a tentative step forward, the soft earth yielding beneath his feet. He reached out a hand, his fingers brushing against the velvety petals of a flower that shimmered with an inner light, its color shifting from deep violet to a dazzling azure. The touch sent a jolt of energy through his body, a pleasant tingling sensation that spread from his fingertips to the crown of his head. He felt a sense of exhilaration, a profound wonder at the beauty and strangeness of this new world.

The path ahead wound through the forest, disappearing into the shadows cast by the ancient trees. He could hear the distant rush of water, a gentle murmur that promised a source of fresh, clean water. He followed the sound, his heart quickening with a mixture of anticipation and a healthy dose of apprehension. This was a world unlike any he had ever imagined, a place where the laws of nature seemed to bend to the whims of magic, where the impossible was commonplace.

As he walked deeper into the forest, the vegetation grew even more bizarre. Trees with pure silver leaves shimmered in the filtered sunlight, their branches adorned with luminous blossoms that seemed to whisper secrets on the breeze. He saw plants that resembled giant mushrooms, their caps glowing with a soft, internal luminescence, casting a light dimly upon the forest floor. Strange, bioluminescent creatures scurried amongst the undergrowth, their bodies emitting a soft, pulsating glow. The air thrummed with an unseen energy, a subtle vibration that seemed to hum in harmony with the rustling leaves and the murmuring stream.

The path led him to a crystal-clear stream, its waters sparkling like a million tiny diamonds in the dappled light. The water tumbled over smooth, moss-covered rocks, creating a gentle cascade that echoed through the silent forest. He knelt beside the stream, cupping his hands to drink. The water was icy cold, yet refreshingly pure, washing away the dust of his old world and the weight of his writer's block. He felt a surge of energy, a revitalization that spread through his body, invigorating him from head to toe.

As he drank, he noticed a reflection in the cool clear water, a reflection that was both familiar and strangely different. His own eyes stared back at him, but there was a gleam in their depths, a spark of something otherworldly, a hint of something magical. He saw hints of strength and determination, traits he had never perceived in himself before. The reflection seemed to pulse faintly, as if mirroring the magical energy surrounding him.

He rose, feeling lighter, more alert, his senses heightened. He had stepped into a world of dreams, a world of magic and wonder, a world that seemed both familiar and utterly alien. The forest was a living entity, ancient and powerful, its silence filled with whispering energy that seemed to reach into his very soul.

Further on, he discovered a clearing bathed in a soft, golden light. In the center of the clearing stood a pool of water, its surface as smooth as glass, reflecting the towering trees and the sky above. The water glowed with an inner light, its surface shimmering with illuminous radiance. He was drawn to it, an irresistible force pulling him towards its luminous depths. He felt a sense of foreboding, a premonition that something significant was about to happen. Yet, the allure of the pool was too strong to resist. He approached cautiously, his heart pounding in his chest, a mixture of excitement and apprehension swirling within him.

As he gazed into the pool's depths, he saw images swirling within the luminous water – fleeting glimpses of landscapes both familiar and strange, faces both known and unknown, scenes of battles and triumphs, moments of joy and sorrow. The images were fragmented, elusive, like half-remember dreams. He felt a connection to this pool, a sense of belonging, as though he had somehow been drawn to this place, to this moment, for a reason he could not yet comprehend.

He extended his hand, his fingers brushing against the surface of the water. The water felt strangely warm, almost alive. He leaned closer, his reflection distorted by the shimmering surface. The images within the pool grew clearer, more defined, but still just out of reach, like a dream just slipping away. He felt a powerful pull, an irresistible force drawing him into the depths. He hesitated for only a moment before plunging his face into the cool embrace of the magical waters, the world dissolved around him in a symphony of lights.

He gasped, his lungs burning, his body convulsing. He felt a searing pain, a sharp, tearing sensation that seemed to rip through his very being. He lost consciousness, collapsing onto the soft grass beside the pool, the world fading to black. Darkness enveloped him, and he slipped into an abyss of oblivion, the whispers of the forest fading into the void. The shimmering light of the magical pool faded as darkness consumed him completely. The sounds of the enchanted forest disappeared, replaced by an overwhelming silence, a profound nothingness that promised both an end and a new beginning. He was lost, but perhaps, in this loss, he would find himself.

The darkness wasn't absolute. It throbbed with a faint, internal light, like the embers of a dying fire. Then, gradually, the blackness began to recede, replaced by a hazy, indistinct luminescence. He felt a gentle pressure, a weightlessness that defied gravity. Slowly, his senses began to return, the world resolving itself from a blurry chaos into something... different.

He wasn't in the clearing anymore. The air, once vibrant with the scent of flowers and damp earth, was now filled with the smell of ozone and something else, something ancient and earthy, like the scent of deep woods after a storm. He was lying on a bed of moss, soft and yielding beneath him, the ground sloping gently upwards. Above him, the canopy was denser, the light filtered through a thick, interwoven tapestry of leaves, creating an almost twilight atmosphere.

He sat up, his head swimming, his body aching. He looked around, his gaze slowly adjusting to the dim light. He was in a grove, smaller than the clearing he'd previously occupied, enclosed on all sides by towering trees whose branches seemed to writhe and twist like living things. The air hummed with an unseen energy, a low thrumming vibration that resonated through the very ground beneath him.

And then he saw her. She stood at the edge of the grove, bathed in a celestial light that seemed to emanate from her very being. She wasn't entirely human. Her form was fluid, shifting and changing as he watched. Her lower body resembled the trunk of an ancient tree, its bark gnarled and textured, its surface covered in moss and lichen. Her upper body, however, was undeniably human, though her features were almost too perfect, too heavenly, to be entirely real. Her skin had the texture of polished ivory, her eyes were the color of moss agate, deep and knowing, and her hair flowed around her like a river of liquid moonlight. She was a creature of paradox, a being that defied easy categorization, a haunting blend of nature and humanity.

She didn't speak in words. Instead, her voice resonated within him, a deep, resonant hum that seemed to vibrate in his very bones. It was a language that bypassed his ears, communicating directly to his soul.

"The pool... it calls to those who are lost, those who seek... answers," the voice echoed within him, the words imbued with both warning and invitation. "But it shows only what it wills, and what it withholds can be as deadly as what it reveals."

He tried to speak, to ask questions, but his voice caught in his throat. The majestic figure seemed to anticipate his questions.

"You are not the first to cross the veil," the voice continued, "nor will you be the last. The threads of destiny are woven into the fabric of existence, some stronger, some weaker. Yours, traveler, is unexpectedly strong."

The figure took a step closer, her movements graceful and fluid, like the swaying of branches in a gentle breeze. She raised a hand, her fingers long and slender, tipped with what looked like polished jade. She gestured towards the path he had come from.

"The path you've walked is fraught with peril, even to one such as you. Aldar's shadow falls long across Coron. His sorcery is a blight upon this land, twisting life into grotesque parodies of its former glory. Morack, his champion, will stop at nothing to break this land."

Her voice held a note of sadness, a deep empathy for the plight of Coron. He wanted to inquire about Aldar, Morack, about the seemingly impossible task that lay before him. But the words seemed to falter, trapped in the weight of the situation.

"But hope remains," she continued, her voice taking on a note of encouragement. "Within you lies a strength you haven't yet discovered, a power waiting to be unleashed.

The prophecy speaks of a writer, a weaver of worlds, who will turn the tide of this dark war on this land."

She paused, her gaze piercing him, her eyes seeming to see into the very depths of his being.

"The pool... it showed you glimpses, fragments of what is to come. It attempted to overwhelm you with the weight of the future; a future you must embrace." Her voice dropped to a near whisper. "Do not be afraid of what you may become, for within you lie the strength of Coron's hope."

She gestured again, this time toward the path leading deeper into the forest. "The Sanctuary awaits. There you will find allies, strength, and answers, but remember this: trust not all that you see, for appearances deceive."

With that, she began to fade, her form dissolving into the shadows of the grove, leaving behind only the lingering scent of ozone and damp earth. The humming in the air intensified for a moment before fading, leaving behind an eerie silence.

He was left alone, the ethereal woman's words echoing in his mind. The prophecy, the looming threat of Aldar, the power he hadn't known he possessed...it was all overwhelming, a dizzying cascade of information that threatened to crush him. Yet, beneath the fear and uncertainty, a new sense of purpose began to bloom. A purpose rooted not in the mundane world he'd left behind, but in this fantastical realm, in the fight for the survival of Coron.

He stood up, his legs trembling, and looked at the path before him. The forest seemed darker now, the shadows deeper, more menacing. The weight of responsibility, the enormity of the task ahead, was palpable. He was no hero, just a writer, lost and bewildered in a strange land. But he was also the one chosen, the weaver of worlds who held the key to Coron's survival. He took a deep breath, a breath filled with the ancient scent of the woods, and began to walk, his steps hesitant at first, but growing stronger and more confident with each stride. His journey had only just begun. The path wound through the forest, deeper into the heart of Coron, towards the Sanctuary, and the destiny that awaited him. He needed to understand his role and his strengths. He needed to believe in himself, in the power that this strange land had awakened within him.

As he walked, he noticed strange, glowing fungi lining the path, their light pulsating faintly. The trees seemed to watch him, their ancient bark whispering secrets in the rustling wind. The very air hummed with energy, a current that flowed around him, fueling his newfound resolve. He was no longer just Gerald Weaver, the struggling writer. The journey was perilous, yes, but within him, a spark of hope burned bright, a flame ignited by a dreamlike encounter and fueled by the destiny that lay before him. He would become something more, maybe a champion, a protector, and the hope of a kingdom teetering on the brink of destruction. The path was long and uncertain, filled with dangers both seen and unseen, but he would walk it, for Coron, for himself, and for the future that awaited him in this strange, magical land. His destiny was intertwined with Coron's, and he wouldn't let it fall. He pressed onward, leaving the grove and the memory of the airy woman behind, the only guide being the sensational hum of magic.

His thirst had become unbearable. A dryness, deeper than any desert sun could inflict, clawed at his throat. He stumbled towards the pool, its surface shimmering like a thousand captured stars. The water itself pulsed with an iridescent light, a slow, rhythmic breathing that seemed to mirror the beat of his own racing heart. He knelt, the moss cool beneath his knees, and cupped his hands, scooping up the shimmering water. It felt strangely warm, almost alive, as it flowed over his parched lips.

The taste was unlike anything he'd ever experienced. It wasn't merely water; it was a symphony of flavors, a complex blend of sweet berries, sharp citrus, and something else, something ancient and earthy, like the scent of the deep forest floor after a storm. As he drank, a wave of energy surged through him, a powerful current that seemed to flow through every vein, every fiber of his being. Images, fragmented and chaotic, flooded his mind: swirling nebulae, clashing armies, faces both familiar and alien, a vast, intricate tapestry of events unfolding before him in a dizzying display of light and shadow.

He saw himself, not as he was, but as something else entirely, a strategist planning intricate battles, a leader rallying desperate souls to fight against insurmountable odds. He saw Coron, a kingdom of breathtaking beauty, besieged by an army of shadows, its people fighting for survival against an encroaching darkness. He saw a sorcerer, powerful and cruel, his face a mask of icy malice, weaving spells of destruction and chaos. He saw a dwarf, small but fierce, her courage, a beacon in the encroaching darkness, her laughter a counterpoint to the looming shadows of war. He saw faint images of faces etched with both worry and hope, waiting for him, for his arrival, his intervention.

The visions were overwhelming, a torrent of information that threatened to break his mind. He felt the weight of centuries pressing down on him, the burden of a destiny he hadn't chosen, a responsibility he wasn't sure he could bear. The images, though vivid, were fleeting, disappearing as quickly as they'd arrived, leaving behind only a residue of intense emotion, fear, and wonder, a sense of profound purpose, and an overwhelming sense of dread.

Beneath the surface of the pool, he saw something, a swirling vortex of energy, a pulsing heart of power that seemed to connect to the very fabric of reality. It was as if the pool was a gateway, a conduit to other worlds, other dimensions. The power that emanated from it was raw, untamed, almost frightening in its intensity. It felt ancient, older than time itself, a force that resonated deep within his soul. And then, darkness.

The world dissolved into a black void, a suffocating emptiness that swallowed him whole. He felt himself falling, tumbling through an endless chasm of nothingness, his senses overwhelmed by a dizzying rush of sensations. The taste of the water lingered on his tongue, a bittersweet reminder of the power he'd briefly glimpsed, the destiny he now carried within him.

When consciousness finally flickered back, he was enveloped in a gentle darkness. He wasn't in pain, but a profound exhaustion weighed him down, each breath a monumental effort. He felt a soft texture beneath his cheek, the moss, he realized, the same moss that lined the banks of the magical pool.

He pushed himself up, his body weak and trembling, and looked around. The pool, still shimmering with its otherworldly glow, seemed to pulsate with a life of its own. The air crackled with unseen energy, a low hum resonating through the very ground beneath his feet. The trees surrounding the pool appeared taller, their branches stretching towards the sky like the arms of ancient beings. Everything seemed... larger, more significant, imbued with a sense of mystery and wonder.

He could feel the lingering effects of the water heightened awareness, a sensitivity to the world around him that was both exhilarating and terrifying. He felt connected to the forest, to the very earth beneath his feet, as if the boundary between himself and the natural world had somehow dissolved. The air hummed with a vibrant energy, a force that coursed through his veins.

He felt... different. Stronger, somehow. More alive. Yet, there was an unnerving awareness of the immense task ahead. The weight of Coron's fate pressed down on him, a heavy cloak of responsibility he had never anticipated.

The images from the pool swirled back into his mind—the vision of Coron under siege, the faces of those who needed him, the prophecy that linked him to their survival. It was a weight he felt in his very bones, a knowledge embedded deep within his being.

He stood, swaying slightly, and looked towards the path leading deeper into the forest. He knew he couldn't stay here. He had to find the Sanctuary. The whispers of the forest, the hum of magic in the air, guided his steps. The magical pool had opened a door, not just to a new world, but to a new destiny, even though he had no idea what awaited him. He filled with a mix of apprehension, excitement, and resolve. The path beckoned, the destiny was clear. The adventure, the responsibility, the hope of Coron – it all began here, by the shimmering, lifegiving pool. He took one step, then fainted into an abyss of darkness.

The gentle darkness yielded to a soft, diffused light. His eyes fluttered open, and he found himself lying on a bed of woven reeds, the scent of chamomile and lavender filling his nostrils. The air was cool and clean, a stark contrast to the heavy, humid atmosphere of the enchanted forest. Above him, a low, vaulted ceiling was adorned with intricate carvings of swirling vines and mythical creatures, bathed in the soft glow of unseen light sources. He was in a room, small but exquisitely crafted, the walls made of polished stone that seemed to hum with a quiet energy. He sat up slowly, his muscles aching, his head swimming with the lingering aftereffects of the magical water. He looked around, taking in his surroundings. The room was sparsely furnished but elegant. A small table stood near the bed, upon which sat a crystal goblet filled with clear water, its surface shimmering with the same faint luminescence he'd seen in the pool. Beside the table, a low, comfortable chair was drawn up, as if someone had been sitting there recently.

A soft footstep echoed from the doorway, and a woman entered the room. She was tall and slender, with hair like spun moonlight and eyes the color of a twilight sky. Her face was framed by a delicate silver circlet, and she wore a long flowing robe of midnight blue, embroidered with silver threads that shimmered in the soft light. She carried herself with an air of quiet authority, a serene grace that belied a strength he sensed rather than saw.

"You are awake," she said, her voice as soft and melodious as a forest stream. "Welcome to the Sanctuary of Lost Souls." He stared at her, speechless. The name resonated with a strange familiarity, as if he'd heard it whispered in his dreams. "I... I don't understand," he finally managed to say, his voice raspy from disuse. "Where am I?"

The woman smiled gently. "You are safe, now. You were found near the Whispering Pool. It seems you've... journeyed far."

She introduced herself as Elara, one of the keepers of the Sanctuary. She explained that the Sanctuary was a hidden haven, tucked away deep within the enchanted forest, a place of refuge for those who had somehow crossed between worlds, travelers like himself, lost and displaced from their own realities. She spoke of others who had found their way to the Sanctuary, each with their own unique story, their own reasons for being there. Some had been adventurers, other scholars, artists, and even children, all bound together by their improbable journeys and their shared need for sanctuary.

Elara explained the Sanctuary's history, a tapestry woven from myth and legend. It was founded centuries ago, a place where the veil between worlds was thin, a place where the lost could find shelter and solace. She described its hidden location, protected by ancient magic and shielded from the prying eyes of the outside world within the Kingdom of Coron. Its existence was known to few, a secret guarded closely by those who served within its hallowed walls. The sanctuary had many chambers, each devoted to a different purpose. There were rooms for healing, libraries filled with ancient texts, meditation chambers for restoration, and workshops for those with skills to share and develop.

As she spoke, a young man entered the room. He was a bit shorter in height to Elara but possessed a more rugged physique, his dark brown hair slightly tousled, his eyes a piercing shade of emerald, green. He had a calm demeanor but a watchful gaze. He carried himself with an aura of quiet strength and competence. He looked at Gerald with a mixture of concern and curiosity. "Finn," Elara said, "This is Gerald. He's new."

Finn nodded in acknowledgement. "Welcome, Gerald," he said, his voice deeper and more resonant than Elara's. "We've been expecting you."

His words, though seemingly straightforward, held an undercurrent of something more profound, a sense of foreboding that tugged at Gerald's instincts. The expectation he felt in Finn's tone was disturbingly significant. He questioned the implications of being 'expected,' sensing a weight of unknown responsibility. It was a strange feeling. He didn't understand how these people knew of his arrival, or why they seemed so certain of his purpose.

Elara and Finn spoke of Coron, the fantastical kingdom Gerald had glimpsed in his visions. They revealed that it was under siege, its people fighting for survival against Aldar, a powerful being who sought to conquer all realms. His reign of terror was a brutal one; conquering lands, enslaving peoples, and leaving behind only ruin and despair. His master sorcerer was Morack, a powerful and merciless sorcerer renowned for his dark magic and cruelty. Morack wielded a force that could not be underestimated.

They told him of the prophecy, an ancient foretelling that spoke of a stranger arriving from another world, a person who would play a crucial role in Coron's defense. A person who held the power to sway the balance of this catastrophic war. A person who, they believed, was him.

"The Whispering Pool chose you, Gerald," Elara explained softly. "It's a gateway between worlds, and you are the latest traveler to find your way here. Your arrival is no coincidence; it's part of a much larger, long awaited destiny."

Gerald felt a surge of adrenaline, a mix of fear and excitement. He was a stranger to this place of uncertainty. His reality had been utterly shattered. The world had changed. The life he had known had been completely overturned. He was suddenly a key figure, not in a story he was writing, but in one that was unfolding around him.

The Sanctuary, despite its inherent serenity, buzzed with a subtle sense of urgency. The keepers spoke of the preparations underway, of the strategy for approaching the Black Forest and scouting Aldar's forces. They discussed the risks involved, the dangers they would face, and the challenges ahead. They spoke of alliances, resources, and possible outcomes, creating a comprehensive battle plan that Gerald would play a vital part in.

As Gerald listened, the gravity of the situation sunk in. The battle for Coron wasn't just a fight for land and power; it was a fight for the very soul of the kingdom, a struggle against a darkness that threatened to consume everything in its path. And he, Gerald Weaver, the struggling writer, was somehow at the heart of it all. The magnitude of what lay ahead would be daunting, yet, strangely, exhilarating, and he was determined to meet this unexpected destiny head on. He felt a surge of determination, a quiet resolve that surprised even himself. The fate of Coron, it seemed, was at hand.

2

Unveiling the Prophecy

The fire crackled merrily in the hearth, casting dancing shadows on the stone walls of the Sanctuary's main chamber. Elara, her moonlight hair catching the flickering flames, gestured towards a large tapestry depicting a swirling vortex of colors, a chaotic blend of landscapes and celestial bodies. "This," she began, her voice low and resonant, "depicts the Great Convergence, the event that birthed the Sanctuary centuries ago."

She explained that the Sanctuary wasn't merely a refuge; it was a nexus, a point where the veil between worlds thinned, allowing for accidental – or sometimes intentional – crossings. The tapestry depicted moments of this convergence; shimmering portals opening and closing, figures flitting between realities, glimpses of worlds both familiar and utterly alien. These weren't just artistic flourishes; each image represented a real event; a historical record etched into the fabric of the Sanctuary's very being.

"The Sanctuary wasn't built; it was... discovered," Finn added, his voice a deep counterpoint to Elara's melodic tones. He leaned against a nearby pillar; his emerald eyes fixed on the tapestry. "Long ago, a group of mages, sensing the instability in the weave of reality, found this place. They realized its potential – its power – and dedicated their lives to safeguarding it."

Finn spoke of the original Keepers, lineage passed down through generations, each keeper possessing a unique blend of skills and abilities. Some were powerful warriors, skilled in combat and strategy, others were adept mages, wielding the subtle arts of manipulation and protection. Some possessed skills in healing, and others in crafting items useful in their tasks of protecting the realm. The Keepers' responsibilities extended far beyond simply sheltering those who stumbled through the rifts between worlds. They were guardians, protectors of a delicate balance, ensuring that the crossings remained infrequent and controlled, preventing catastrophic breaches that could unravel the fabric of reality itself.

"The Whispering Pool," Elara continued, her gaze drifting towards Gerald, "is the most potent gateway here. It chooses those it deems worthy, or perhaps... necessary." Her words hung in the air, heavy with unspoken meaning. She described how the pool's magic identified individuals destined to play significant roles in the realms it connected. These weren't always heroic roles; sometimes, those chosen were unwitting catalysts for change, their actions triggering events with far reaching consequences.

Finn explained that the current crisis in Coron was no accident. Aldar, in his insatiable quest for power, had been manipulating the convergence points, creating larger, more unstable rifts to facilitate his conquest of neighboring realms. He was using dark magic to amplify the energy flow between worlds, exploiting the inherent instability to his advantage. This reckless act not only threatened Coron but also risked a catastrophic collapse of the dimensional barriers, a cosmic event that could shatter the very foundations of existence.

"The prophecy speaks of a Bridgebinder," Elara revealed, her eyes meeting Gerald's. "Someone who can mend the fractured threads of reality, someone who can restore balance to the convergence points and ultimately defeat Aldar."

Gerald felt a shiver crawl down his spine. He was no hero; he was a writer, accustomed to crafting stories, not living them. Yet, the words hung in the air like an inescapable truth. He did not portray himself as a Bridgebinder. The prophecy hadn't just predicted his arrival; it had summoned him.

The Keepers then revealed more about the history of the Sanctuary itself, sharing ancient texts and legends. They spoke of a time before the Sanctuary, when the crossings between worlds were more frequent and unpredictable. The chaos that ensued – the battles between beings from different dimensions, the merging of realities that led to unimaginable consequences – had nearly destroyed the very fabric of existence.

They detailed the intricate magical systems within the Sanctuary, designed not only to protect the refugees but also to monitor and control the flow of energy between worlds. They showed Gerald intricate diagrams of dimensional rifts, explaining how they fluctuated in strength and how the Sanctuary's magic served as an anchor, a stabilizing force.

They revealed the Sanctuary possessed an ancient library, a vast repository of knowledge spanning countless realities. The library held texts describing the histories of other worlds, detailed accounts of battles fought between interdimensional beings, and prophecies and legends that stretched back to the dawn of time. The texts were written in various languages, many of which were long since extinct, and some were written in languages beyond human comprehension. The library alone was a testament to the Sanctuary's age and its crucial role in preserving the balance of reality.

Elara described her own role in the Sanctuary: protecting it through defensive measures, preparing for the coming battle. She spoke of utilizing her powerful magic as a Mage. She further spoke of Finn, with his mastery of ancient lore and his strategic mind when it came to protecting Coron.

The conversation stretched into the night, the flickering firelight painting their faces in shifting hues. Gerald, initially overwhelmed, began to grasp the enormity of his task. He began to realize; he may be the key to protecting not just one kingdom, but the delicate balance of existence itself. The weight of responsibility seemed immense, but so was the potential for heroism. The destiny that awaited him was hanging in the balance. The quietness of the Sanctuary, once a comfort, now seemed to resonate with the pulse of an unfolding destiny, a cosmic drama in which he was both the observer and the protagonist. The night ended, not with rest, but with a renewed sense of purpose and the dawning realization of the journey that lay ahead.

Elara produced a worn leather-bound book, its pages brittle with age. The cover, adorned with intricate silver filigree, depicted a stylized sun sinking beneath a mountainous landscape, a single crimson star blazing in the twilight sky. "This is the Book of Coron," she whispered, carefully opening it to a page filled with arcane symbols and faded illustrations. The air itself seemed to hum with a low, resonant energy as she began to decipher the ancient script.

The prophecy, she explained, was not a simple prediction of the future, but rather a tapestry woven from time itself, its threads interweaving past, present, and future. They were not mere embellishments; each depicted a significant event, a key moment in Coron's long and turbulent history. One illustration showed a vast, worldly battle, celestial beings clashing amidst a storm of cosmic energy. Another depicted a lone figure, cloaked and hooded, standing before a shattered gateway, Aldar a conqueror of death and destruction, The third depicted a person, strikingly similar to you Gerald, a figure with luminous glow, the light radiating from him seemingly holding back a tide of encroaching darkness.

"This," Elara traced a finger across the illustration of the man, "is the Bridgebinder. The prophecy speaks of a being from another world, a writer of tales, who will arrive at a time of great peril. He will be the key to sealing the rifts Aldar is creating, and in doing so, he will determine the fate of Coron, and perhaps many other worlds."

Finn, his gaze fixed on the intricate script, added, "The prophecy is riddled with riddles and ambiguities. The language is archaic, its meaning veiled in metaphors and symbolism. Generations of Keepers have attempted to fully interpret its cryptic warnings, but the true extent of its implications remains unclear until now. However, there's no doubt Gerald about your role in this. The symbols surrounding the figure matching your likeness are unmistakable."

Elara continued, her voice low and intense. "The prophecy speaks of a trial, a series of tests that the Bridgebinder must face. These trials are not merely physical challenges but tests of character, of spirit, of the very essence of who he is. Each trial reveals a new aspect of the Bridgebinder's power, a new facet of his destiny, revealing his capacity to protect not only Coron but the very fabric of existence." She pointed to a specific symbol, a swirling vortex surrounded by what looked like shattered shards of glass. "This represents the Great Rift, the main point of vulnerability in the dimensional barriers. Aldar seeks to widen it, to tear apart the fabric of reality. Only the Bridgebinder can mend it."

The pages turned, revealing a series of increasingly detailed illustrations. One showed a vast, sprawling army, banners bearing the symbol of Aldar's serpentine crest fluttering in the wind. Another showed a desperate battle, Coron's defenders fighting valiantly against overwhelming odds. Still others showed scenes of devastation, landscapes ravaged by dark magic, cities reduced to smoldering ruins. The visual descriptions within the book were almost painfully realistic, depicting horrors that could have only been witnessed by someone who had seen the events firsthand.

The illustrations, Elara explained, were not mere artistic representations. They were imbued with the very essence of the events they depicted, fragments of memory, echoes of fought battles, and tragedies endured. The images flickered, their colors shifting and swirling, as if the scenes themselves were attempting to break free from their ancient confines.

Finn added that some sections of the prophecy were written in a language unknown even to the wisest Mages of the Sanctuary, implying that this knowledge was beyond the comprehension of the Coronians, implying a far older and more mysterious origin than previously imagined. This language, he speculated, might be a language of pure energy, a form of communication that transcended the limitations of spoken tongues.

Elara smiled faintly. "The prophecy doesn't offer explicit instructions. It's more of a roadmap, a series of clues that will guide the Bridgebinder. Each trial faced will reveal a greater understanding of his powers, his connections to the Sanctuary, and the nature of the threat posed by Aldar."

Finn added, "The prophecy hints at the existence of ancient mystical incantations, so powerful that could be used to enhance the Bridgebinder's abilities and turn the tide of the battle. Their location is obscured by cryptic clues, enigmas only revealed once the Bridgebinder has overcome various challenges and trials."

Elara continued, "The prophecy also warns of betrayals. Not all allies are trustworthy; even those who appear steadfast in their loyalty may harbor hidden agendas, influenced by Aldar's dark magic." She glanced meaningfully at Gerald. "You must be vigilant, Gerald. Trust your instincts but be wary of those who seek to exploit you for their own gain. Not all who seem to offer aid are working in your best interest."

The pages of the book turned, revealing an even more detailed picture of the coming battle and Gerald's role. They spoke of specific locations within Coron, places of ancient power, that would be crucial to the defense. The Black Forest, already identified as a crucial staging area for Aldar's forces, would be a focal point of one conflict, the scene of numerous skirmishes. The prophecy detailed the movements of Aldar's armies, predicting strategic maneuvers, ambushes, and counter offensives.

As they delved deeper into the prophecy, the illustrations became increasingly vivid, almost three dimensional. The symbols pulsed with light, seeming to hum with a faint energy, resonating with the very emotions and events they depicted. Gerald felt a strange connection to these images, a feeling of familiarity despite the alien nature of the world and its history. It was as if he was not just reading about these events; he was living them, experiencing them through the very fabric of the ancient text.

The final page of the book depicted a climactic battle, a confrontation between the Bridgebinder, Morack and Aldar's forces. The Bridgebinder, depicted as a figure of immense power, radiant with light, stood against a backdrop of swirling chaos, facing a shadowy figure emanating an aura of pure malevolence. The outcome was unclear, left deliberately ambiguous, a testament to the uncertainty of the future and the choices that would need to be made.

As Elara closed the book, a palpable silence fell over the Sanctuary. The weight of the prophecy, the immensity of the task ahead, was unsettling to Gerald. He had entered a fantastical world; he was the linchpin in a cosmic struggle, a destiny woven into the very fabric of reality itself. The fire in the hearth crackled, casting elongated shadows on the stone walls, while the weight of expectation hung heavily in the air, a prelude to the battles that lay ahead. The reality sets in, he was the Bridgebinder, and the fate of Coron, and perhaps many other worlds, were dependent upon him. His path now was paved with prophecy, peril, and the promise of a destiny he never knew existed.

The air in the Sanctuary, thick with the weight of the prophecy, crackled with a newfound energy. Elara, her face etched with a mixture of worry and determination, gestured towards a shadowed corner of the room. From the darkness, a figure emerged, small but undeniably formidable. This was Falon, a female dwarf whose stature belied her strength and spirit. Her dark eyes, sharp and intelligent, assessed Gerald with a mixture of curiosity and skepticism. Her braided hair, interwoven with tiny silver beads, cascaded down her back, framing a face both youthful and weathered by the harsh realities of life in Coron.

Falon wore leather armor, intricately tooled and adorned with small, but clearly effective, enchantments. A quiver of arrows, crafted from dark wood and tipped with obsidian, hung at her side, and a finely crafted crossbow, its metal gleaming faintly, was strapped securely to her back. From her leather belt hung a small but sharp battle axe. She carried herself with confidence that suggested years of experience navigating the treacherous landscapes and perilous encounters of Coron. Her skills were invaluable; she had the ability to repair equipment, creating intricate traps, and employing guerilla warfare tactics with deadly efficiency. She possessed knowledge that would greatly benefit the planned incursion into Aldar's forces, and she was an excellent scout. Falon's knowledge and skills were essential to Coron.

"So, this is the 'Bridgebinder'," Falon said, her voice a husky whisper that carried an undercurrent of doubt. She didn't quite look at Gerald, instead scrutinizing him from beneath lowered brows. "He looks... ordinary. Not exactly what I pictured when they spoke of a savior."

Her skepticism was palpable, a stark contrast to the reverence with which Elara and Finn had treated the prophecy. Falon's pragmatism, honed by years spent battling the harsh realities of life in a war-torn kingdom, was a refreshing counterpoint to the ghostly aura that surrounded the prophecy. She represented a more grounded approach to the imminent threat, a welcome change from the often mystical and vaguely unnerving tone of the Keepers.

"He may look ordinary, Falon," Elara replied gently, "but the prophecy speaks of hidden strengths, untapped potential. His arrival is no coincidence. His presence here is crucial to our survival."

Falon grunted, unconvinced. "Prophecies are full of riddles and double speak. I've heard enough of those blasted things in my lifetime. I believe in what I can see, touch, and wield. And right now, all I see is a man who stumbled out of some hole in the ground and is apparently meant to save our world. Show me the proof." She crossed her arms, her gaze unwavering.

"The proof is in the coming trials, Falon," Finn added, his voice measured. "The prophecy outlines a series of tests. Each one will reveal more about Gerald's capabilities, forging him into the hero Coron needs."

Falon's expression remained dubious, but a flicker of curiosity – perhaps even a hint of grudging respect – flickered in her eyes. "Trials, huh? I like trials. They're much more reliable than vague prophecies. I've faced enough in my years to know what a real challenge looks like, and I know how to meet it." She gave Gerald another assessing glance. "But this one, he might need a little... coaching." Elara smiled slightly. "Falon will be your guide, Gerald. She knows the Black Forest better than anyone, and her combat skills are unmatched. She'll help you prepare for what lies ahead."

"Prepare?" Gerald asked, his voice still tinged with the disorientation of his sudden arrival in Coron. The concept of trials and the sheer scale of the looming threat were still sinking in. "Prepare for what, exactly?"

Falon smirked. "Prepare for a war, that's what. A war against an evil being and a sorcerer who conquered other realms. War is coming, I assure you of that." She took a few steps towards the map of Coron laid out on the table, its detailed contours indicating the formidable terrain of the kingdom. Her finger traced the border between the relative safety of the Sanctuary's location and the dark expanse of the Black Forest.

"Aldar's forces are gathering in the Black Forest, preparing for a massive assault on Coron's capital," she explained, her voice taking on a grave tone. "We need to scout their position, determine their strength, and identify their weakness. And it goes without saying, if we get to take a few scalps while we're at it, then all the better."

"The Black Forest is treacherous," Elara cautioned. "It's steeped in ancient magic, haunted by creatures of nightmare, and teeming with Aldar's spies. But, if we can gain intelligence before their assault, we can buy ourselves precious time."

"Time is what we don't have," Falon countered. "We need to be swift and decisive. We'll need a strategy and the strength to pull it off. Gerald, this is where you come in. What are you good at? Besides writing."

Gerald hesitated. His writerly instincts might not be much use in a war, but his mind worked quickly, adapting to his impossible situation. "I... I'm a quick study," he stammered, choosing a vague response. "And I'm good at observation. And I'm certainly not afraid of a challenge, whatever form it may take."

Falon raised an eyebrow. "That's a start. But I need more than words. I need results. We leave at dawn. Prepare yourself, Bridgebinder." She turned and vanished into the shadows, leaving behind a tangible sense of determination and no small amount of fear. It was now crystal clear – Gerald's role wasn't just about prophecies and destinies; it was about survival, and success would depend on his quick learning curve and Falon's expertise in navigating Coron's brutal realities.

The following hours were a blur of preparation. Falon, efficient and practical, oversaw the gathering of supplies: rations, water skins, healing salves, extra arrows, and more than a few suspiciously well-worn daggers. She meticulously checked Gerald's rudimentary equipment, replacing his worn traveling boots with sturdy leather ones and providing him with a basic set of traveler's gear, all sturdy and clearly purpose-built. The Keepers, despite their mystical roles, assisted with practical tasks such as sharpening knives and replenishing oil for the torches.

Falon's instruction was terse but clear. She taught Gerald basic survival skills: how to track, how to use a bow and arrow (despite his initial clumsiness), and how to identify edible plants. She stressed the importance of stealth and observation, skills she possessed in abundance. She explained the dangers of the Black Forest in stark detail, describing the terrifying creatures that lurked within its shadows: Wraiths that fed on fear, thorny vines that ensnared the unwary, and nightmarish beasts with eyes that glowed in the darkness. The details, drawn from her own experiences, were far more terrifying than any prophecy.

As dawn approached, Gerald felt a mixture of dread and exhilaration. He was no longer just a writer escaping a writer's block; he was becoming a soldier, a scout, a vital component in the defense of a kingdom he barely knew. He understood now that the trials Elara had spoken of weren't simply metaphorical tests of character; they were actual life or death encounters in a world where magic was as real as the blood that would inevitably be spilled.

As they stepped out of the Sanctuary, into the pale light of the early morning, Falon fell into step beside him. Her gaze was intense, not unkind, but certainly unforgiving.

"Listen closely, Bridgebinder," she said, her voice low. "In the Black Forest, there is no room for error. Your life, and the fate of Coron, depend on your ability to adapt, to learn, and to survive. Now, let's go. We have a war to prepare for."

The journey into the Black Forest was a harrowing test of endurance. The trees, ancient and gnarled, seemed to bask in the gloom, their branches like skeletal fingers reaching out to grasp them. The air hung heavy with the scent of damp earth and decaying leaves, and a palpable sense of dread settled upon them. Falon moved through the forest with effortless ease, her knowledge of the terrain allowing them to navigate the labyrinthine pathways with confidence, avoiding the many traps and dangers the forest held. Gerald, however, struggled to keep pace, his every step a cautious dance in a world he didn't understand.

Their initial scouting mission yielded chilling results. They encountered Aldar's scouts, shadow clad figures moving with unnatural speed and silence. The skirmishes, though brief, were brutal. Falon's skills with a crossbow were unmatched, her arrows finding their mark with deadly accuracy. Gerald, while initially clumsy and fearful, showed an unexpected resilience, adapting quickly to his new role as an unlikely warrior.

He wasn't strong, but he was fast, and his keen observation skills, honed from years of meticulous detailed work in his stories, allowed him to identify hidden paths and anticipate the enemy's movements. He learned quickly how to read the language of the forest: the rustle of leaves, the snap of a twig, the subtle shift in the shadows – all indicators of unseen dangers and potential ambushes. Falon watched him with a growing respect, her initial skepticism gradually giving way to a grudging admiration for his adaptability and determination.

As the sun dipped below the horizon, casting long, menacing shadows, they retreated, carrying with them valuable intelligence about Aldar's forces – their strength, their location, their tactics. They had survived their first attempt, a brutal introduction to the realities of the coming war. But it was just the beginning. The path ahead remained treacherous, shrouded in uncertainty, but with Falon's guidance and Gerald's rapidly evolving skills mimicking Falon. The prophecy's path was now unfolding, and they were ready for whatever came next.

On their return to the Sanctuary the flickering torchlight cast long, dancing shadows on the faces of Elara and Finn as they recounted the encounters in the Black Forest. Their voices, normally soft and measured, held a tremor of fear, a testament to the gravity of the threat they faced. The air in the sanctuary, already heavy with the weight of the prophecy, seemed to grow colder and denser, as the full extent of Aldar's power was revealed.

"Aldar began subtly disguised as a savior," Elara explained, her voice barely a whisper. "Aldar, a skilled manipulator, he used intrigue and cunning alliances to consolidate his power. But then... we discovered he was not what he seemed. He showed a source of immense dark magic. It amplified his innate abilities through his sorcerer called Morack, twisting his ambitions into something monstrous."

Finn nodded, his gaze fixed on the map of Coron, his finger tracing the borders of the kingdom, a silent acknowledgment of the vulnerability they faced. "His conquest wasn't merely a series of military victories. He doesn't merely conquer lands; he corrupts them, twisting the very essence of their being, their magic, their people, to serve his twisted will."

He paused, letting the chilling implications of his words sink in. "The realms he's subjugated... they're not merely conquered; they're broken, their vibrant ecosystems withered, their inhabitants enslaved or turned into twisted parodies of their former selves. Their magic, once a source of life and wonder, is now warped, fueling Aldar's insatiable hunger for power." Falon leaned forward, her dark eyes burning with a fierce intensity. "So, he's not just an ambitious warlord. He's a necromancer, a plague upon the very lands he touches. He drains life from everything he conquers, leaving behind only ashes and despair." She paused, her expression grim. "And he's coming for Coron." Elara continued, her voice low and grave. "Each realm he conquered, he's absorbed its power. His dark magic grows exponentially with each victory. Imagine a parasitic vine, wrapping itself around a tree, draining its life force, growing stronger with every drop of sap it absorbs. That is Aldar. He feeds on the very essence of the realms; his strength becoming immeasurable." Finn added, "His power is unlike anything we've ever encountered. It's not just about brute force or cunning strategy: it's about twisting the very laws of nature to his will. He commands legions of shadow creatures, creatures born from the corrupted magic of the conquered realms. They are relentless, tireless, fueled by a darkness that chills the soul."

"And Morack," Falon added, her voice laced with a chilling undertone. "His sorcerer, Morack. He's Aldar's right hand. A master of illusions and deception, his mind control is so potent he can turn even the most loyal warriors against their own kind."

The weight of their words hung heavy in the air. Gerald, still reeling from his sudden arrival in this strange, magical world, felt a surge of fear, but beneath it, a spark of determination ignited. He was no soldier, no warrior, but he was resourceful. He was adaptable. And he was, unexpectedly, part of this fight for survival.

"What can we do?" Gerald asked, his voice barely above a whisper. The enormity of the threat, the sheer scale of Aldar's power, was almost overwhelming.

Elara's gaze met his, her eyes reflecting the fire of hope amidst the despair. "The prophecy speaks of a 'Bridgebinder', You, Gerald, are that Bridgebinder. Your arrival is not merely a coincidence; it is the key to Coron's survival."

"But how?" Gerald asked, desperately seeking a tangible answer amidst the overwhelming threat. "How can I, a writer, possibly stand against such a powerful sorcerer?"

Finn smiled faintly, a glimmer of hope amidst the shadow of fear. "The prophecy is cryptic, but it hints at your potential. Your skills, seemingly unrelated to combat, may prove invaluable. You possess a unique perspective, an outsider's view. And you have a strength we haven't mentioned yet...your creativity. Your mind, adept at constructing worlds of fiction, may be what's needed to unravel Aldar's magic."

Falon interrupted. "Enough with the riddles. We need a plan, a solid strategy. We know Aldar's forces are gathering. We know their strength. We've identified their weaknesses. Now, we need to use that knowledge to our advantage. We need to strike before they strike us."

Her words sparked a surge of renewed determination in the room. Elara, Finn, and Gerald exchanged glances, a silent acknowledgment of the shared burden, the daunting task that lay before them. This wasn't a battle of armies; this was a struggle against a power that threatened the very fabric of reality. And the outcome would depend not only on their combined strength, but on Gerald's ability to harness his unexpected talents in this fantastic war.

The following days were a whirlwind of activity. Falon, with her unparalleled knowledge of the Black Forest, meticulously mapped out Aldar's encampments and supply lines. Gerald, drawing on his skills of observation and his keen attention to detail, helped in identifying patterns in Aldar's movements, providing crucial insights that complemented Falon's military perspective. He found himself surprisingly adept at strategizing, his creativity translating into novel tactical plans that surprised even Falon with their ingenuity. His writer's mind, previously used to crafting intricate narratives and believable characters, now found a new purpose—devising strategies to outwit a ruthless sorcerer and his army of shadow creatures. He analyzed Aldar's previous conquests, searching for patterns, weaknesses, and subtle clues that could reveal his methods and vulnerabilities. He spent hours looking over ancient texts in the Sanctuary's library, researching Aldar's history and the magic he wielded, hoping to find a chink in his formidable power.

The Keepers provided him with arcane knowledge, ancient spells, and prophecies, guiding him through the complex web of magical lore that surrounded Aldar's power. He learned of the symbiotic relationship between Aldar and his magic, how his power fed on the despair and destruction he wrought, and how disrupting this cycle could potentially weaken him. This newfound knowledge fueled Gerald's determination even further, giving him a sense of purpose beyond mere survival; he was now fighting for the survival of Coron and all the realms threatened by Aldar.

His initial fear gave way to a steely determination. He trained relentlessly with Falon, improving his archery, stealth techniques, and honing his reflexes. While he may not have been a natural warrior, his eagerness to learn, combined with his sharp intellect and unwavering resolve, made him an invaluable asset to the team.

As the final preparations were underway tension filled the Sanctuary. The threat was imminent, palpable in the hushed whispers and determined gazes of the Keepers and Falon. Gerald, gazing at the map of Coron, saw not just a map of a kingdom, but a battleground, a canvas for a conflict that would determine the fate of countless lives. The battle for Coron was about to begin, and Gerald, the unlikely Bridgebinder, was ready to play his part.

The air filled with the odor of dank, dark decay filled the air as they stood at the edge of the Black Forest, reminding everyone of the dangers that exist. A wall of ancient, gnarled trees, their branches intertwined like skeletal fingers, stretched before them, disappearing into an oppressive gloom that seemed to swallow the light itself. The silence was unnerving, broken only by the occasional rustle of unseen creatures and the distant, mournful cry of a bird. This was no ordinary forest; this was a place of shadows and secrets, a realm where magic pulsates with dark energy.

Falon, her dwarven face grim, adjusted the quiver on her back, her hand resting on the hilt of her axe. "The Black Forest," she murmured, her voice barely audible above the rustling leaves, "is a labyrinth of twisted paths and ancient magic. It's a place where the line between reality and illusion blurs, where the very trees seem to watch you, judging your every move."

Elara, her eyes scanning the dense undergrowth, nodded. "Many have ventured into the Black Forest, but few have returned. It's guarded by creatures of nightmare, twisted by Aldar's corrupting influence. We must move with caution, relying on our senses and our training."

Finn, his eyes alight with an uncanny intensity, added, "The forest itself is alive, a sentient entity, its moods as unpredictable as the storms that rage within its depths. It can be both a barrier and a guide, depending on how you approach it."

Gerald, his heart pounding in his chest, felt a shiver run down his spine. He was a writer, accustomed to creating worlds of fantasy, but this was no fiction. This was real, visceral, and terrifyingly tangible. The sheer weight of the impending danger pressed down on him, a burden of responsibility. He was part of this mission, a vital cog in a desperate plan against an overwhelming threat.

Falon produced a small, intricately carved wooden compass. "This," she explained, "was crafted by an ancient cartographer, a master of the Black Forest's arcane pathways. It will help us navigate through the maze, but it will only guide us to the outskirts of Aldar's main encampment. Beyond that, we're on our own." She handed the compass to Gerald, and he held the cold, smooth wood in his hand, feeling a strange sense of connection to this ancient artifact, a conduit to the forest's secrets.

They began their trek into the forest's heart, the darkness pressing in on them from all sides. The air grew heavy, thick with a sense of foreboding. Every rustle of leaves, every snap of a twig, sent a jolt of adrenaline through Gerald, sharpening his senses, heightening his awareness.

As they ventured deeper, the forest changed. The trees grew taller, their trunks thicker, their branches more intertwined, forming a dense canopy that blotted out most of the light. Strange, phosphorescent fungi glowed eerily from the mossy trunks, casting an unsettling green light on their surroundings. The air grew colder, and the silence, previously unnerving, now felt suffocating.

They encountered strange, unsettling creatures. Whispering willows, their branches swaying with unnatural grace seemed to beckon them closer, only to withdraw as they approached. Shadow wolves, their forms indistinct in the dim light, stalked them from the darkness, their eyes glowing like embers. Giant spiders, their bodies the size of hounds, spun webs of shimmering moonlight, their sticky threads glistening like dew laden spider silk. Each encounter was a test of nerves, a trial of skill, and a reminder of the forest's malevolent nature.

Gerald, armed with his bow and arrows, found himself surprisingly adept at navigating the treacherous terrain. His writer's mind, accustomed to intricate plots and strategic twists, helped him anticipate the forest's subtle shifts and traps. He quickly mastered stealth techniques, learning to blend into the shadows, moving with a fluidity that surprised even Falon. His writer's imagination transformed into a tactical advantage, his ability to visualize potential dangers and plan counterstrategies proving invaluable.

One evening, while they were resting near a secluded stream, Finn warned them of a creature called the Gloom Stalker, a shadowy entity that fed on fear and despair. It was said to possess the ability to manipulate the forest's darkness itself, creating illusions and trapping its victims in endless labyrinths. Its presence was signaled by a chilling silence, a void of sound that was more frightening than any roar or shriek. He urged them to remain vigilant, to trust their instincts and avoid any sense of unease or panic.

During their journey, they discovered ancient ruins – remnants of a civilization swallowed by the forest long ago. The stones, covered in strange carvings and symbols, seemed to hum with magical energy. Elara, with her knowledge of ancient lore, identified them as the remains of a city that once flourished in the heart of the Black Forest, a city corrupted and ultimately destroyed by Aldar's dark magic. The ruins served as a stark warning, a testament to the forest's power and Aldar's ruthless ambition.

As they drew closer to Aldar's main encampment, they encountered more of Aldar's forces. Shadow creatures twisted mockeries of nature, stalked the forest floor, their eyes burning with a malevolent fire. They were relentless, tireless, driven by an insatiable hunger for destruction. Gerald, drawing on his newfound skills, helped the group to avoid detection, utilizing the forest's cover and his keen observational abilities to outwit their pursuers.

Finally, they reached the outskirts of the encampment. From their concealed position, they observed Aldar's army, a terrifying spectacle of shadow creatures and corrupted soldiers. The sheer scale of his forces was overwhelming, a chilling testament to his power. But amidst the darkness, they also saw signs of vulnerability, chinks in his seemingly impenetrable armor. The knowledge they gathered would prove crucial in the battle to come. They had successfully scouted Aldar's forces, but their mission was far from over. The Black Forest had yielded its secrets, but a far greater challenge lay ahead, a challenge that would determine the fate of Coron and perhaps, all realms threatened by Aldar. The return journey would be equally perilous, but they now had the knowledge they needed to plan their next move and face the approaching battle with a renewed sense of hope and determination.

3

The Bridgebinder
Trials

The air grew colder as they plunged deeper, the scent of decaying vegetation replaced by a chilling dampness that seeped into their bones. The phosphorescent fungi, initially eerie, now seemed menacing, their sickly green glow casting long, distorted shadows that danced and writhed like living things. The trees themselves seemed to press in on them, their gnarled branches reaching out like skeletal arms, their leaves whispering secrets in a language they couldn't understand.

They encountered a creature unlike anything Gerald had ever imagined. It resembled a giant, iridescent spider, but its body was composed of shifting shadows and moonlight, its eight legs ending in razor sharp claws that glinted in the dim light. Its eyes, two fiery red , seemed to pierce through the darkness, fixing on them with an unnerving intensity. It moved with an unnatural grace, its shadow body rippling and flowing like liquid darkness. Falon, with a battle cry, launched herself forward, her axe whistling through the air, but the creature vanished in a puff of moonlight, reappearing behind them with startling speed. Its attack was swift and precise, its claws slashing at Finn, leaving a deep gash on his arm. Elara, with her staff alight with a protective spell, managed to fend off the creature, forcing it to retreat into the shadowy depths of the forest.

The incident left them shaken. The creature's ability to manipulate shadows and moonlight was unlike anything they had encountered before, a testament to the forest's uncanny and dangerous magic. The sense of unease deepened, the forest's hostility seeming to intensify with each passing hour.

As they continued their mission, they stumbled upon a clearing, in the center of which stood a towering oak, its branches reaching towards the sky like supplicating arms. The tree pulsed with an unnaturally energy, its leaves shimmering with an ethereal light. As they approached, they heard a voice, soft and melodious, yet filled with ancient sorrow. The voice spoke in riddles, its words weaving a tapestry of prophecy and warning. It spoke of Aldar's growing power, of the impending doom that threatened Coron, and of Gerald's crucial role in the battle to come. The voice hinted at secrets hidden within the forest, secrets that could turn the tide of the war, but also warned of the dangers that lay in wait for those who sought them.

The encounter with the talking oak left Gerald profoundly disturbed. The forest seemed to possess a sentience he hadn't anticipated, a capacity for communication and manipulation that went beyond simple magic. He felt a growing sense of unease, a feeling that they were not merely traversing a physical landscape but venturing into a realm of consciousness, a living, breathing entity that observed and judged their every move.

Their path was further complicated by the constant threat of illusions. The forest, manipulated by Aldar's magic, frequently played tricks on their senses, creating false paths and misleading visions. Trees seemed to shift and change before their eyes, paths would vanish into thin air, and familiar landmarks would suddenly appear in unexpected locations. Gerald, relying on his writer's intuition and strategic thinking, helped to navigate these illusions, piecing together the reality from the deceptive tapestry woven by the forest.

One evening, as they sought shelter from a sudden downpour, they found themselves trapped in a cavern, its walls adorned with ancient carvings that depicted a civilization battling monstrous creatures. The carvings told a story of a once great kingdom, consumed by the forest's darkness, destroyed by Aldar's precursor, a sorcerer of immense power who had ruled the land centuries ago. The story echoed the prophecy the oak had spoken, indicating that the cycle of destruction and rebirth was repeating itself. They also discovered evidence of other travelers who had ventured into the Black Forest – remnants of campsites, scattered equipment, and the ghostly remains of fires long extinguished. The evidence spoke of desperation and defeat, serving as grim reminders of the dangers that lurked within the forest's depths. Each discovery fueled a growing sense of dread, highlighting the immense challenge they faced.

The deeper they went, the more pervasive Aldar's influence became. They encountered contorted, corrupted versions of forest creatures – giant, shadow like wolves with eyes of burning coal, birds of prey with obsidian feathers that swooped down from the darkness, and tree creatures with gnarled branches that moved with a terrifying purpose. They were relentless, relentless in their pursuit, driven by a dark will that transcended mere instinct.

As they neared Aldar's encampment, the forest itself seemed to change. The trees grew taller, their branches intertwined, creating a suffocating canopy that blocked out most of the light. The air grew heavy, thick with an almost palpable sense of malice.

They discovered a hidden path, concealed behind a waterfall, leading to a vantage point overlooking Aldar's encampment. From their hidden position, they witnessed the full extent of Aldar's power. His army was vast and terrifying, a legion of shadow creatures and corrupted soldiers, their numbers seemingly endless. But amongst the darkness, Gerald observed a pattern, a vulnerability in Aldar's defenses, a weakness he suspected could be exploited.

Their experiences within the Black Forest was transformative. Gerald, the writer, had stepped into his own story, and the lines between reality and fiction had blurred beyond recognition. The journey had been perilous, but the knowledge they gained, the understanding of Aldar's forces. The

Black Forest had tested them, pushed them to their limits. The return would be just as perilous, but they carried within them the hope of victory, and the knowledge that they were prepared to face whatever lay ahead.

The path ahead twisted and turned, the trees themselves seeming to shift and writhe, their branches like grasping claws. The air thrummed with energy, a potent cocktail of magic and malice that prickled their skin. Suddenly, a monstrous shadow detached itself from the gloom, its eight legs ending in wickedly curved blades glinting in the dim light. It was a colossal spider, easily the size of a small carriage, its carapace a shimmering tapestry of midnight blue and iridescent green. Its many eyes, glowing with evil intellect, focused on them with predatory intent.

Falon, the warrior, roared a challenge, her axe whistling through the air as she launched a furious attack. The spider, however, was impossibly fast and agile. It weaved through Falon's blows with contemptuous ease, its legs a blur of motion. One swipe grazed her arm, leaving a searing burn that quickly blackened and blistered. Elara, her staff a blazing beacon, countered with a volley of spells, forcing the creature to retreat, its many eyes flashing with irritation. But the beast wasn't merely powerful; it was intelligent, its movements suggesting a cunning tactical mind. It retreated only to reposition itself, utilizing the tangled undergrowth to its advantage.

Gerald found himself strangely calm in the face of this terrifying creature. His writer's mind, he began to analyze the spider's movements, looking for patterns, weaknesses, and potential strategies. He noticed a slight hesitation in its movements whenever Elara's spells impacted on its legs. A chink in its seemingly impenetrable armor.

He shouted his observation to Elara, suggesting a coordinated attack focusing on its legs. Elara, ever quick to adapt, adjusted her spells, targeting the spider's vulnerable extremities with precise bursts of magical energy. Falon, taking her cue, concentrated her attacks on the same areas, her axe striking true each time. The spider, its mobility hampered, became less agile, its attacks less forceful. With a final, concerted effort, they brought the gigantic arachnid down, its massive body collapsing with a heavy thud that resonated through the forest.

Their victory, however, was short lived. As they moved along, they encountered a creature of far more unsettling nature. It didn't stalk them like the spider; it seemed to become the forest itself. One moment, it was a gnarled, twisted tree trunk, the next, a swirling vortex of leaves and branches. It morphed seamlessly from one form to another, sometimes appearing as a towering, menacing figure, other times as a slithering serpent of living vines. Its shifting form made it nearly impossible to attack effectively.

This shapeshifter was a master of illusion, twisting the very fabric of the forest to its will. It toyed with their senses, creating false paths and misleading visions, mirroring their deepest fears and insecurities. For Gerald, it manifested as a terrifying vision of his unfinished manuscript, pages filled with gibberish, his characters rendered as twisted, grotesque parodies of themselves. Each faced their deepest anxieties, their inner demons unleashed in a horrific display of psychological warfare.

The battle was waged not with steel and magic, but with resolve and clarity. Gerald, drawing upon his experience as a writer, focused on the narrative structure of the shapeshifter's illusions. He realized the illusions were tied to their emotional vulnerabilities. By confronting their fears openly, by acknowledging and accepting them, they weakened the shapeshifter's power, forcing it to revert to a more stable form. Once they had identified and overcome their psychological barriers, the creature's power waned, leaving it vulnerable to Elara's attack.

Exhausted but victorious, they stumbled forward, only to face another seemingly insurmountable challenge. The forest floor ahead opened into a vast clearing bathed in eerie twilight. From the shadows, a creature of immense size and power emerged: a colossal forest cat, its fur the color of midnight, its eyes like pulsating fiery orbs. This was no ordinary feline. Its size alone was terrifying, its lithe, powerful body capable of unleashing devastating force. Its claws were like scimitars, and its teeth glistened menacingly. It stood silently, its massive form exuding an aura of predatory intensity, a danger that froze them in their tracks.

This guardian, unlike the others, demanded respect rather than conquest. It didn't attack relentlessly; it tested them. It observed their movements, their reactions, their ability to work together. It challenged them to prove their worthiness, to demonstrate that they were not simply intruders, but deserving allies.

Elara, sensing the creature's intentions, approached slowly, offering no hostility, no threat. She spoke softly, her voice clear and measured, explaining their purpose, their quest to protect Coron. Falon, although wary, kept her axe sheathed, understanding that a battle here might be more devastating than any they had faced before. Gerald the observer, watched carefully, trying to decipher the subtle cues in the creature's posture and demeanor.

The great cat observed them for what felt like an eternity. Its amber eyes studied them intently, assessing their courage, their trustworthiness. Finally, with a slow, deliberate movement, it lowered its head, offering no attack but a clear sign of acceptance. The creature's demeanor shifted, its aura softening from one of predator to protector.

It seemed that this guardian didn't want to destroy them but test their readiness to face the coming conflicts. They had proven their teamwork, their resilience, and their ability to overcome adversity. They had faced their fears, both real and illusory, and emerged stronger. The forest cat, a sentinel of the Black Forest, nodded once, acknowledging their passage. The perilous journey through the heart of the forest continued. They had overcome the guardians, but the true battle lay ahead. The threat of Aldar and his formidable army loomed large, the shadow of their coming confrontation casting a long and ominous presence. The Black Forest, with its threatening guardians and perilous trials, had prepared them for the daunting challenges that awaited them, shaping them into the unlikely heroes that Coron needed. The journey continued, the forest floor, a treacherous tapestry of gnarled roots and decaying leaves, offered little respite. Each step was a calculated risk, a test of balance and agility. Falon, however, moved with an almost unnatural grace, her small frame a whirlwind of controlled motion. She navigated the treacherous terrain with the practiced ease of someone intimately familiar with the forest's hidden pathways. Unlike Gerald and Elara, who stumbled and occasionally lost their footing, Falon seemed to anticipate every obstacle, her feet finding secure purchase on the uneven ground. Her dwarven heritage, honed through generations of life in the mountainous regions bordering the Black Forest, gifted her with a remarkable sense of balance and an instinct for navigating difficult landscapes.

Her ears, finely tuned to the subtle sounds of the forest, picked up the softest creaks of shifting branches, the whispers of unseen creatures lurking in the shadows. This acute awareness was far beyond that of a mere woodsman; this was the honed perceptiveness of a seasoned warrior, perpetually vigilant and prepared for any threat.

Several times, she warned them of impending danger, her sharp cries alerting Gerald and Elara to hidden pitfalls or camouflaged predators. Once, she spotted a viper, its emerald scales perfectly blending with the mossy undergrowth, coiled and ready to strike. With a swift, almost imperceptible movement, she deflected the snake's attack, her axe flashing in a blur of motion, dispatching the reptile before it could even fully uncoil. She did this without breaking stride, the act appearing almost effortless.

Her skills extended beyond mere evasion. She possessed a remarkable knowledge of the forest's flora and fauna. On several occasions, she identified edible plants, providing a much-needed boost of energy and sustenance. She also knew which plants to avoid, recognizing poisonous varieties with a practiced eye. Her understanding of the forest's ecosystem was profound, enabling her to anticipate the behavior of its creatures and predict their movements.

This knowledge wasn't simply theoretical; it was a practical skill born of countless hours of observation and experience. She could identify tracks with incredible precision, differentiating the prints of various creatures with practiced ease. She could interpret the signs of the forest – the broken branches, the disturbed earth, the scent of animals carried on the wind – to piece together the story of the landscape, deducing the movements and intentions of both beast and predator.

The forest itself seemed to test Falon's abilities. One particularly challenging section involved navigating a treacherous ravine, the path barely wider than a person's shoulders, with a sheer drop on either side. The wind howled through the gap, whipping at their clothes, and a misty rain slicked the rocks, making the ascent perilous. Gerald and Elara struggled, their movements hesitant and unsure, several times nearly losing their footing. Falon, however, moved with surprising speed and confidence, her small size giving her an advantage as she squeezed through narrow passages and maneuvered around unstable rocks. She even helped

Gerald and Elara, supporting them as they negotiated the treacherous climb.

Their movement through the Black Forest was a continuous exercise in adapting to unexpected circumstances. They faced dense thickets, navigating through tangled undergrowth that snagged their clothes and hampered their movement. They traversed bogs, sinking occasionally into the mucky earth, their progress slowed. Falon used her axe to clear paths, her powerful strokes felling small trees and chopping through thick brush, creating trails for the group to follow. Her expertise transformed the near impassable terrain into a navigable route, enabling them to move forward, ever deeper, into the heart of the forest.

But the challenges weren't just physical. The forest was imbued with dark magic, a pervasive sense of unease that preyed on their minds. It manipulated their senses, creating illusions and playing tricks on their perception. Gerald, being the writer, found it particularly disorienting, as images from his unfinished novel – distorted and menacing – began to overlay his perception of reality. This heightened sense of unease and the mental fatigue of facing such illusions were nearly overwhelming. Elara, with her magical abilities, worked to clear away the illusions, but the cumulative effect of the dark energy was challenging to combat.

Falon kept the group anchored, her practicality grounding them amidst the chaos. She was a steadfast presence, her confidence and focus helping Gerald and Elara maintain their composure and continue their arduous journey.

There were times when Falon's skills saved the entire party from dire circumstances. They were once ambushed by a pack of vicious wolflike creatures, their eyes glowing with predatory hunger. These were no ordinary wolves; they were imbued with dark magic, larger and more ferocious than any natural beast. Falon's quick thinking and strategic positioning played a critical role in their escape. She used her knowledge of the terrain to lead them through a maze of trees, using the undergrowth as cover and taking advantage of the creatures' limited visibility. While Elara created a diversion with fire spells, Falon deftly guided them to safety.

As they forged through the dark heart of the forest, they encountered a strange, illuminous fog that distorted their perception of time and space. This fog wasn't simply an atmospheric phenomenon; it was a magical construct, warping reality. It caused disorientation, blurring the line between illusion and reality. Falon managed to guide them through the fog. Even the forest's dark magic, which seemed to affect Elara and Gerald more keenly, held little sway over Falon, who navigated the eerie mists with remarkable clarity.

She constantly encouraged Gerald and Elara, bolstering their morale and helping them push through moments of despair and doubt. Her unwavering spirit acted as a beacon of hope in the oppressive darkness of the Black Forest, reminding them of their purpose and giving them strength to continue.

The Black Forest had tested them to the extreme.

As they ventured onward, the more oppressive the silence became. Even Falon, usually so alert and perceptive, seemed subdued, her usual cheerful demeanor replaced by a thoughtful gravity.

They came across a clearing, oddly devoid of vegetation. The earth was bare, scorched black as if struck by lightning. In the center stood a single, gnarled oak, its branches twisted into grotesque shapes, its bark etched with otherworldly symbols that seemed to writhe and shift before their eyes. Elara, her eyes narrowed in concentration, cautiously approached the tree. She touched the bark, her fingers tracing the strange carvings. A faint hum vibrated through her hand, a low vibration that resonated deep within her bones. "This is... unsettling," she murmured, drawing back her hand. "This magic... it's ancient, powerful, and... corrupted." Gerald, the writer, felt a shiver run down his spine. The symbols looked disturbingly familiar, echoing fragments of dreams he'd had since his arrival in Coron. Vague, half formed images of shadowy figures, twisted landscapes, and a looming, obsidian tower flickered at the edges of his consciousness. He struggled to grasp their meaning, to translate the subconscious language into concrete understanding. The feeling was akin to stumbling upon a forgotten, half buried manuscript – tantalizing hints of a larger narrative but obscured by the passage of time and the ravages of decay. Falon, meanwhile, was examining the ground. She pointed to several small, bonelike fragments scattered around the base of the tree. "These aren't animal bones," she said, her voice low. "They're... humanoid. And they're not fresh."

Elara knelt beside her, examining the fragments closely. "They're incredibly old," she confirmed, her brow furrowed. "The magic here... it's preserving them, somehow. But not in a lifegiving way. It's more like... mummification."

The discovery sent a fresh wave of unease through the group. The sheer scale of his actions, hinted at by these seemingly insignificant remnants, was terrifying. This wasn't merely an invasion; it was a desecration.

As they continued their journey, they found more evidence of Aldar's activities. Hidden amongst the trees, they stumbled upon a makeshift encampment, hastily abandoned. Scattered around the clearing were remnants of supplies, broken weapons, and the disturbingly preserved bodies of what appeared to be grotesque creatures – hulking beasts with reptilian features and glowing, crimson eyes. They looked almost deliberately preserved, as if serving a specific purpose rather than simply being victims of conflict.

Elara cautiously examined the creatures' remains. "These are... creations," she whispered, her voice barely audible. "They're not natural. They've been... crafted."

Aldar wasn't just using existing creatures; he was creating new, more terrifying ones. The scale of his power, his control over the very essence of life and death, became brutally apparent. He started to understand the true threat to Coron but potentially to all the realms.

Further into the forest, they discovered a hidden cavern, its entrance obscured by a veil of shimmering mist. Within, they found a series of intricate carvings etched into the cave walls – maps, diagrams, and symbols depicting rituals and magical formulas. Falon recognized some of the symbols; they were related to ancient dwarven lore, but corrupted, twisted into something dark and sinister.

The carvings revealed details of Aldar's plans. He was planning a large scale assault on Coron's capital, utilizing a devastating magical weapon powered by the very essence of his sorcerer Morack.

The forest, however, offered little respite. They encountered creatures warped by Aldar's magic – twisted versions of forest animals, their bodies grotesquely altered, their eyes burning with unnatural light. These beings were no mere beasts. Each encounter was a brutal struggle, a testament to the corrupting force of Aldar's magic.

They were forced to fight their way through, Elara's magic providing a crucial advantage, but even her skills were stretched to their limit. Falon's axe found its purpose, and her dwarven strength and resilience kept them moving forward. The secrets of the Black Forest were beginning to reveal themselves, unveiling not just Aldar's power but also potential avenues for his downfall. The oppressive silence of the Black Forest continued, broken only by the occasional snap of a twig underfoot or the rustle of unseen creatures in the undergrowth. The air heavy with the scent of rotting vegetation and something else... something acrid and metallic. They pressed on, their senses heightened, each footstep measured and deliberate. The feeling of being watched, a constant companion since entering the deeper reaches of the forest, intensified.

Suddenly, Falon stopped, her hand raised. "Wait," she whispered, her voice barely heard above the rhythmic drumming of their own hearts. She pointed towards a dense thicket of thorny bushes, their leaves a sickly yellowish green. "There's a path," she murmured, peering into the tangled undergrowth. "Hidden. Almost invisible."

Elara and Gerald cautiously approached, their eyes scanning the thicket. It was almost imperceptible, a barely discernible break in the dense vegetation, a subtle shift in the pattern of shadows.

"It's unnatural," Elara observed, her fingers tracing the edge of the hidden passage. "The magic here... it's weaving the illusion, making the path invisible to the casual observer." She touched the thorny bushes, her fingers brushing against something smooth and cold beneath the spines. "Stone," she whispered, her voice filled with wonder. "The path is carved from stone, concealed by a magical illusion."

As they ventured onto the hidden path, the oppressive atmosphere shifted subtly. The air, though still heavy with foreboding, felt... different. It was as if they had crossed an invisible threshold, entering a realm within a realm. The sounds of the forest, muffled before, became clearer, more defined.

The path wound its way through the forest, leading them further into its heart. They passed towering trees; their branches intertwined like skeletal vine of bones reaching for the sky. The light was muted, filtered through a dense canopy that created an ethereal twilight, casting long, dancing shadows that seemed to sway and shift like living beings.

The path itself seemed to guide them, subtly curving and twisting, as if possessed of a will of its own.

After what seemed like hours, they emerged into a wide, open clearing. Before them lay another of Aldar's encampment, a scene of stark contrast to the surrounding forest. It was not a haphazard collection of tents and makeshift shelters, but a meticulously organized military base, carved from the very heart of the forest. They blended into the dark forest, almost invisible, yet at the same time strangely imposing.

The size of the encampment was staggering. Hundreds, perhaps thousands, of soldiers moved with precision and purpose, their movements orchestrated like a well-rehearsed dance. They were not just ordinary soldiers, but creatures warped and twisted, their forms grotesque and unnatural. Some were hulking brutes, their skin like hardened leather, their eyes glowing with a malevolent crimson light. Others were more lithe and agile, their bodies serpentine and sinuous, their movements swift and silent as shadows.

The sheer number of these creatures, their grotesque appearance, and the chilling efficiency of their movements sent a wave of fear through Gerald. This wasn't just a military encampment; it was a hive of swarming energy, a nexus of dark magic, pulsating with a terrifying power.

Elara, her eyes narrowed in concentration, scanned the encampment, her hands resting lightly on the hilt of her sword. "The layout... it's strategic," she murmured. "It's designed to maximize the use of the forest itself as a weapon."

The encampment was cleverly positioned to exploit the forest's natural features – ravines, dense thickets, and treacherous bogs. The soldiers were not merely stationed; they were integrated into the landscape, using its natural defenses to their advantage. It was a testament to Aldar's tactical brilliance, his ability to harness not just magic, but the environment itself, to create an impregnable fortress.

Falon, her eyes scanning the structures, noticed something unusual. "The buildings... they're not made of stone," she whispered. "They're made of something else... something organic."

As they got closer, they discovered that it seemed to be composed of interwoven roots and branches, twisted and molded into the shape of buildings, its surface gleaming like polished cold black ice.

This discovery gave them a chilling insight. The entire encampment was a testament to his power, a horrifying demonstration of his control over life and death.

As the sun began to dip below the horizon, casting long shadows across the clearing, they made the difficult decision to withdraw. They had much to plan, much to discuss. The battle for Coron would be far harder than they could have imagined, but now, with this newfound knowledge, they could begin to revise their plans into a solid a strategy. They needed to return to the Sanctuary and reveal their findings.

4

Scouting the Enemy

On a clearing at the top of nearby ravine, it offered another view to the immense size of Aldar's forces. It wasn't the mere size that struck them – though the sheer scale was breathtaking, a sprawling complex that seemed to devour the forest itself – but the unsettling atmosphere that emanated from it. A sense of dread hung in the air, a miasma of dark magic woven into the very fabric of the place.

From their hidden perch, nestled amongst the gnarled roots of an ancient oak, they observed the relentless activity within the encampment. Thousands of soldiers, or rather, twisted parodies of soldiers, swarmed like insects, each movement precise and unnervingly efficient. They weren't human, not entirely. Some resembled hulking beasts, their skin like cracked earth, their eyes glowing with an unnatural crimson fire. Others were more serpentine, their limbs elongated and sinuous, moving with the fluid grace of predators. Their armor, if it could be called that, was crafted from the very substance of the forest – dark, almost living metal that seemed to pulse with an inner light. It was as though the forest itself had been corrupted, twisted into a weapon against Coron.

The sounds of the encampment were a cacophony of unsettling noises. The rhythmic clang of metal on metal, the guttural roars of the larger creatures, the sibilant whispers of the serpentine soldiers – all combined to create a terrifying symphony of chaos and preparation. They heard the rasping of unseen machinery, the grinding of gears, the eerie hum of dark energy – a sound that resonated deep within Gerald's chest, echoing the unease that had gripped him since their arrival in the Black Forest.

The obsidian-like structures, which Falon had correctly identified as living, organic matter, dominated the landscape. They were not merely buildings; they were grotesque imitations of the forest's own growth, dark, twisted parodies of trees and roots, contorted into imposing fortresses. The structures pulsed with a faint, internal luminescence, a sickly green glow that seemed to leach the color from the surrounding forest. It was as if the very lifeblood of the woods was being drained, fueling the horrifying growth of Aldar's war machine.

Between the structures, a network of pathways, carved from the same dark, living material, crisscrossed the encampment. Along these pathways, teams of soldiers moved with an almost mechanical precision, transporting supplies, preparing weaponry, and engaging in drills that seemed designed to maximize their brutality and efficiency. They carried weapons that looked like twisted versions of nature itself: scythes forged from petrified wood, bows fashioned from the bones of monstrous creatures, and spears tipped with sharpened obsidian, seemingly imbued with dark magic.

Elara, her gaze sharply and focused, noted the strategic placement of the encampment. "Aldar has chosen this location for a reason," she murmured, her voice barely a whisper. "The ley lines here... they are incredibly powerful." She pointed towards a particular section of the encampment, where a massive, pulsating orb of dark energy emanated from one of the larger structures. "That is the heart of it all. He's tapping into the raw magical energy of the forest, using it to amplify his own power, to empower his army."

Falon added her own insights. "The organic material... it's constantly growing, changing. It's not just a building material; it's a living weapon, evolving, adapting to any threat." She pointed towards a group of soldiers who seemed to be inspecting a section of the wall that had been damaged. "They're repairing it... but not with tools. They're using their bare hands, manipulating the living substance, almost as if they were growing it back."

Gerald, despite his initial fear, found himself captivated by the unsettling spectacle. The sheer scale of Aldar's ambition, the terrifying display of his power, was almost breathtaking in its audacity. It was a ritual; a dark sacrament performed to harness the power of the forest and twist it to Aldar's will.

The hours passed, and as twilight descended, casting long, ominous shadows across the encampment, the activity intensified within. A sense of urgency pervaded the air, a feeling that some significant event was imminent. They watched as a contingent of soldiers, distinguishable by their more grotesque appearances and their weaponry, gathered around the central, pulsating orb. They performed a ritualistic dance, chanting in a language Gerald didn't understand, but whose sinister tone sent a chill down his spine.

The ritual culminated in a surge of dark energy that rippled outward from the orb, engulfing the soldiers in a wave of malevolent power. When the energy subsided, the soldiers looked different, larger, stronger, their eyes glowing with an even more intense crimson light. They were clearly enhanced, empowered by Aldar's dark magic, transformed into something more monstrous, more deadly.

As the first stars began to appear in the darkening sky, the size of Aldar's army, his sophisticated strategies, and the horrifying nature of his creatures left little room for optimism. Yet, they would not be deterred. They would find a way to fight back, to defend Coron, even against such seemingly overwhelming odds

As they continued their observation, a figure emerged from the central structure, a figure that commanded instant and chilling attention. He was tall and gaunt, his robes the color of a raven's wing, embroidered with symbols that seemed to glow and shift before their eyes. His face was pale, almost skeletal, his eyes burning with an infernal light that seemed to pierce the darkness itself. This was Morack, Aldar's chief sorcerer, the architect of their nightmares.

His presence sent a wave of dark energy emanating from him that pressed down on them, a tangible weight that seemed to suffocate the very air around them. Even from their hidden vantage point, the feeling was overwhelming, a suffocating dread that hinted at the immense power he wielded. Falon, instinctively tightened her grip on her axe, a low growl rumbling in her chest. Elara's hand rested on the hilt of her sword, her eyes narrowed in concentration, assessing the threat. Gerald, despite his fear, felt a strange pull towards Morack, a sense of morbid fascination mixed with a profound dread.

Morack moved with an unsettling grace, his movements fluid and precise, as though he were gliding rather than walking. He didn't seem to hurry, yet he covered vast distances with effortless ease. He surveyed the encampment with a critical eye, his gaze sweeping over the ranks of soldiers, the grotesque structures, the pulsating orb of dark energy. He didn't shout orders; his mere presence commanded obedience, a silent authority that permeated the entire encampment.

The soldiers, even the monstrous creations, seemed to recoil slightly at his approach, a show of respect or perhaps fear bordering on worship. Their movements became more precise, their obedience almost robotic as they continued their preparations under his silent scrutiny. Morack's influence was evident in every aspect of the encampment, a sinister undercurrent that linked the disparate elements into a unified, massive force.

He approached the pulsating orb, placing his hand upon its surface. The orb pulsed faster, the dark energy intensified, radiating outwards in waves that rippled through the encampment. The soldiers nearest to the orb seemed to writhe under the surge of energy, their bodies contorting, their forms shifting and reforming. It was a grotesque display of power, a demonstration of Morack's ability to mold and shape the living substance that comprised much of Aldar's forces.

As Morack stood before the pulsating orb, he began to chant in a low, guttural voice, a language that sounded like the rasping of stones grinding together, punctuated by unearthly shrieks that chilled them to their very core. The air around him shimmered and distorted, revealing glimpses of swirling, malevolent energies that seemed to writhe and coil like venomous serpents.

Gerald felt a sudden, sharp pain in his head, a searing sensation that momentarily robbed him of his breath. He clutched his temples, his vision blurring as a wave of dizziness washed over him. The dark energy emanating from Morack seemed to target him, a subtle yet undeniable assault on his mind, a probe into his very being. He gasped, trying to regain his composure, his heart pounding in his chest. Elara and Falon looked at him with concern, but Gerald shook his head, signaling that he was alright, though the lingering headache persisted. This was more than just a feeling of dread; it was an actual attack, a subtle incursion into his consciousness by Morack's malevolent power.

The chanting grew in intensity, the dark energy swirling around Morack, forming a vortex of power that seemed to suck the light from the surrounding forest. The ground beneath them trembled, the very air vibrating with the raw power of the dark magic. The trees seemed to shudder their leaves rustling in an unnatural wind, as though the very forest itself was in agony.

Morack's power was not just magical; it was deeply interwoven with the very essence of the forest, a corrupting influence that contorted nature itself into weapons of destruction. He seemed to be drawing power from the earth itself, harnessing the ancient energies by means of lines that ran beneath the encampment, amplifying his already immense capabilities.

As the chanting reached its crescendo, the air crackled with energy, and a blinding flash of dark light erupted from the orb. The light was so intense that Gerald had to shield his eyes, even from their concealed vantage point. When he could see again, he witnessed a truly horrifying sight. The soldiers gathered around the orb had undergone a complete transformation.

Their eyes glowed with an intense crimson light; their skin seemed to ripple and shift like molten lava. Their weapons, once merely menacing, with dark energy, pulsating with a life of their own.

The sight left them breathless, the sheer terror of the spectacle almost paralyzed. This was no mere army; it was an army of horror, forged in the crucible of dark magic, fueled by the corrupt essence of the forest itself. The implications of what they had witnessed sank deep, confirming the terrifying reality of the battle to come. The sheer scale of Aldar's power, augmented by Morack's dark sorcery, was overwhelming. Yet, they had seen enough. They knew what they had to face, and the gravity of their mission pressed down upon them with renewed intensity. It was time to retreat, to gather their thoughts, to formulate a strategy to combat this seemingly insurmountable foe. Their escape back along the hidden path was a silent, swift retreat, leaving behind the chilling reminder of the power they now faced.

The retreat was tense, every rustle of leaves, every snap of a twig, sending jolts of adrenaline through their veins. They moved silently, their every step calculated, guided by Elara's innate understanding of the forest's hidden paths. Falon's keen eyes scanned their surroundings, her axe held ready, while Finn provided a steady rearguard, his watchful gaze never leaving the shadowed depths of the woods. Gerald, though still reeling from the psychic assault, focused on maintaining his composure, his mind racing to process the horrifying spectacle they had witnessed.

The monstrous creations, the grotesque structures, the sheer raw power emanating from Morack and the pulsating orb – all pointed to a level of dark magic that surpassed anything they had ever encountered. Yet, amidst the overwhelming terror, a flicker of hope ignited in Gerald's mind. He had seen weaknesses, cracks in Aldar's seemingly impenetrable defenses.

First, the dependence on Morack's magic was striking. The army, the structures, even the weapons seemed intrinsically linked to the sorcerer's power. If Morack were incapacitated, the entire army might unravel, the monstrous soldiers reverting to their original, less terrifying forms. This was a significant, albeit risky, point of vulnerability.

Second, the concentration of forces around the pulsating orb and Morack himself indicated a potential vulnerability. While the center of the camp seemed protected, the outer perimeter appeared less heavily guarded. While the monstrous soldiers were terrifying, their movements seemed somewhat clumsy and uncoordinated away from the direct influence of Morack's magic. This suggested that a swift, focused attack on a less defended section of the perimeter might allow for infiltration and sabotage, potentially disrupting supply lines or even causing chaos within the ranks. However, such a tactic would require detailed reconnaissance and the precision of a surgical strike, timed to coincide with a diversionary tactic.

Third, the apparent reliance on dark magic to sustain the monstrous soldiers implied a dependence on a consistent flow of energy. If that flow could be interrupted, even temporarily, it might weaken the soldiers significantly. This suggested that identifying and disrupting the conduits, perhaps by severing the connections through tactical destruction or magical interference, could significantly degrade Aldar's army's fighting capacity.

Fourth, the organic nature of the camp itself presented another potential avenue of attack. The grotesque, pulsating buildings seemed to be both living and consuming dark energy, implying a vulnerability to fire. While fire might be ineffective against the monstrous soldiers themselves, it could be used to destroy the organic structures, reducing the camp's defensive capabilities and potentially disrupting Morack's rituals, denying him a focal point for his power. However, this would require a carefully planned attack, to minimize collateral damage and ensure the safety of the Coronian forces.

Fifth, while the entire army presented a unified front, the sheer size of the encampment implied logistical challenges. Disrupting supply lines, potentially through ambushes or targeted attacks on convoys, could starve the army over time, causing dissent and weakening its capacity for sustained combat. This, however, would require a strategy of patience and persistence, potentially stretching out the conflict over a longer period.

The challenge, however, wasn't just identifying these weaknesses; the scouts needed a detailed strategy, a plan that accounted for every contingency, every possible risk. They would need to use stealth, deception, and perhaps a bit of daring luck. The information they had gathered was crucial, but it was only a piece of a far larger puzzle.

As they finally reached the Sanctuary, exhaustion hanging heavily in the air, they shared their grim findings. Elara, Finn, and Falon listened intently, their faces etched with grim determination. Aldar's forces were formidable, but not invincible. The cracks in his defenses, though subtle, offered a glimmer of hope in the face of overwhelming odds.

The ensuing discussions were long and intense; a war council held under the flickering candlelight of the Sanctuary. They analyzed every detail of their observations, scrutinizing each potential weakness, weighing the risks against the rewards. They debated different strategies, considering the strengths and weaknesses of their own forces. Gerald, despite his limited experience in warfare, surprised them all with his insightful observations, his keen eye for detail picking up on nuances that others had missed.

They realized that any successful attack would require a coordinated effort, a multipronged assault designed to exploit several weaknesses simultaneously. A swift attack on a weak defended section of the perimeter, coupled with a diversionary tactic to draw attention away from a coordinated strike against Morack's energy source or the destruction of the organic structures, would be essential. But this couldn't be a brute force approach; it would require cunning, precision, and the element of surprise.

The planning continued through the night, each detail meticulously examined and debated. They sketched diagrams on scraps of parchment, plotting potential attack routes, calculating the optimal timing for the various phases of their assault. They assigned roles and responsibilities, acknowledging each person's unique skills and strengths. It was a meticulous process, a grim ballet of preparation for an almost certainly perilous battle. The fate of Coron, and perhaps even other worlds, rested on the success of this meticulously planned assault. The task ahead remained monumental, but for the first time, they may have a fighting chance.

5

Preparing for Battle

T he air in the Sanctuary hummed with nervous energy, a palpable tension that crackled between the flickering candlelight and the hushed whispers of strategizing. Elara, her eyes reflecting the dancing flames, unfolded a weathered map of Coron, its intricate details illuminated by the soft glow. Around the table, the weight of their collective responsibility settled heavily. The fate of the kingdom rested on the shoulders of this unlikely band of heroes – a writer plucked from another world, a spirited dwarf, two seasoned keepers of ancient secrets, and the looming shadow of an impending war.

"Aldar's forces are larger than we initially anticipated," Finn stated, his voice low and measured, his finger tracing the lines of the map, indicating the sprawling encampment in the Black Forest. "His siege engines are formidable, and his magical defenses... they are unlike anything I've encountered before."

Falon, being practical, interjected, "His supply lines are surprisingly vulnerable, though. I noticed a gap in their patrols near the Whispering Falls. A swift strike there could disrupt their movement and potentially cripple their advance." Her normally vibrant face was serious, her eyes reflecting the grim reality of the situation. She tapped a specific point on the map, her finger hovering over a narrow valley that snaked through the dense forest. "We could ambush them there, catching them off guard."

Gerald, still grappling with the surreal nature of his circumstances, found himself surprisingly comfortable amidst the intensity of their planning session. He offered, "From what I observed, their formations are rigid, almost predictable. Their reliance on brute force and dark magic leaves them susceptible to well-coordinated attacks that exploit their lack of flexibility." His observations, rooted from his mundane experience of strategic war games from countless books and movies, surprisingly proved insightful in this fantastical setting. He added, "A concentrated assault, timed with a diversion elsewhere, could create chaos and exploit those weaknesses."

Elara nodded slowly, her gaze sweeping across the faces of her companions. "Gerald's insights are valuable. We must use our knowledge of their weaknesses to our advantage. Aldar relies on fear and overwhelming force. We must counter that with precision and cunning." She traced a line on the map, linking Falon's proposed ambush point to a series of smaller, less defended pathways. "We'll need a three-pronged attack. Falon's team will strike the supply lines. A second group, led by Finn, will create a diversion near the main encampment, drawing their attention away from the crucial assault."

Finn, his brow furrowed in concentration, raised a hand. "The diversion needs to be significant enough to be credible yet not so devastating that it risks depleting our resources prematurely. We need to achieve a balance between drawing them out and preserving our strength for the main engagement." He tapped his finger against the map, pointing to a section of the forest known for its particularly dense growth, perfect for concealing smaller units. "We could employ a combination of ambushes and deceptive tactics to make them believe we are launching a full-scale assault from the northern flank. This would draw their forces away from the primary strike."

Elara continued, "While Finn engages the enemy's main forces, Gerald and I will lead the primary strike. We'll focus on weakening their defenses, focusing on disrupting the magical barriers around the compound. Gerald's unexpected presence in this world... is perhaps more significant than we originally believed. There might be a way to exploit this unexpected element." A flicker of something unreadable shone in her eyes – a hint of anticipation, a suggestion of a plan that extended beyond the immediate battle.

The ensuing discussions were intense, a whirlwind of tactical maneuvers, contingency plans, and carefully weighed risks. They dissected Aldar's army, analyzing their strengths and weaknesses with surgical precision. They explored various scenarios, simulating different outcomes, and adapting their strategy to account for every potential setback. The days melted into nights, fueled by strong Coronian ale and an unwavering commitment to their shared cause.

Finn meticulously mapped out the various attack routes, detailing the optimal timings and deployment of troops. He even incorporated specific terrain features—rock formations, ravines, and thickets—into the plan to maximize the effect of their ambush strategy. Falon, drawing upon her deep knowledge of the Black Forest, added crucial details about the terrain, including hidden pathways and blind spots that could be exploited for surprise attacks.

Gerald, though initially overwhelmed, quickly found his niche in the strategic discussions. His unexpected perspective, grounded in the logic of modern warfare simulations, offered a refreshing counterpoint to the Coronians' more traditional approach. He contributed valuable suggestions on communication strategies, focusing on exploiting the gaps in Aldar's communication to ensure that Aldar's forces would be unable to coordinate their response effectively.

Elara, the visionary leader, connected all the elements, weaving together the various tactical considerations into a unified plan. She incorporated the ancient prophecies, interpreting cryptic clues and drawing upon forgotten knowledge to enhance their overall strategy. She emphasized the importance of exploiting the emotional and psychological factors of warfare, suggesting ways to sow discord among Aldar's ranks and undermine his morale.

As the days of meticulous planning drew to a close, a sense of grim determination filled the Sanctuary. The detailed strategy that emerged from the combined wisdom and experience of the group. But even with their meticulous plan, there was a deep understanding of the immense risks they were about to undertake. This was not just a battle; it was a fight for the very soul of Coron. The upcoming battle would test not only their military prowess but also the strength of their bond and the depth of their commitment. The time for preparation was over. The time for battle had arrived.

The air in the Sanctuary, thick with the scent of woodsmoke and anticipation, felt charged with a different kind of energy now. The meticulous planning was complete, the strategy laid out, but the sheer scale of the task ahead demanded more than just their small band. To defeat Aldar, they needed an army. A unified Coron, rising against a common enemy, was their only hope.

Elara, despite the magical nature of her world, addressed the group. "Our plan is sound, but numbers are crucial. Aldar's forces dwarf ours. We need to rally the various factions of Coron, to unite them under a common banner. It won't be easy; years of internal strife have fractured the kingdom, leaving it vulnerable to Aldar's conquest."

Finn, the cautious strategist, nodded. "The clans of the Silver Peaks, traditionally aloof and wary of outsiders, could prove a valuable asset. Their mountain warriors are renowned for their resilience and their skill in guerilla warfare. But their loyalty is fiercely guarded; gaining their trust will require careful diplomacy and a demonstrable show of our strength and resolve."

Falon added, "And then there are the River folk. They are skilled boatmen and archers, well versed in the marshlands that border the kingdom. Their knowledge of the terrain is invaluable. However, they are suspicious of all outsiders, especially those from the uplands."

Gerald, surprised by his growing familiarity with the intricacies of Coronian politics, suggested, "Perhaps we could leverage the shared threat of Aldar to bridge the divides. A common enemy can be a powerful unifying force. We could demonstrate our commitment to the defense of Coron, showcasing our success in disrupting Aldar's supply lines, as proof of our capabilities and determination."

Elara smiled, a flicker of admiration in her eyes. "An excellent suggestion, Gerald. It's time to show them the strength of our alliance."

Their first stop was the Silver Peaks. Gerald and his three companions gathered their gear. The journey was arduous, a perilous trek through treacherous mountain passes, the biting wind and icy slopes testing their endurance. The peaks themselves seemed to exude an ancient, almost mystic, power. The air was thin, and the silence, broken only by the occasional cry of a hawk, was almost deafening. Finally, they reached the stronghold of Clan Stonehand, nestled high amidst the jagged peaks. The clan leader, a grizzled warrior named Borin Stonehand, was initially hesitant. He greeted them with cautious scrutiny, his eyes sharp and perceptive, his posture rigidly defensive.

Elara, with her natural charisma and diplomatic skill, explained their plan, emphasizing the shared threat of Aldar and the importance of uniting against a common enemy. She spoke of their intent in disrupting Aldar's supply lines, of the precision of their strategy, and of their unwavering commitment to the defense of Coron. Finn, supplemented Elara's words with detailed tactical assessments, emphasizing the practicality of their alliance. He highlighted the strategic advantages that the Stonehand clan's mountain warfare expertise could bring to the overall plan.

Falon, with her straightforward and honest demeanor, charmed the warriors with her tales of daring escapades and battlefield exploits. She also demonstrated her remarkable craftsmanship by showing them one of her intricate traps, an ingenious design that was both elegant and lethal. Gerald, despite his initial anxieties, found himself surprisingly confident. He presented his analysis of Aldar's military strategy, highlighting the vulnerabilities in his seemingly impenetrable army.

Borin Stonehand, initially resistant, was gradually won over by the strength of their argument and the evident commitment of this unlikely alliance. He admired their strategic thinking, their determination, and their shared resolve. He saw in them not just a group of warriors asking for his help, but a force capable of turning the tide of the war. After much deliberation, and witnessing the evident skills of the group, he agreed to pledge his warriors to their cause. The clan would provide a crucial flanking force, attacking

Aldar's rear lines, creating havoc and chaos amongst Aldar's army.

Their next destination was the marshlands that bordered the kingdom, home to the River Folk. The journey was different this time, a slow and careful navigation through treacherous swamps and winding waterways. The River Folk, a people as enigmatic as the marshes they called home, were initially wary of these unexpected visitors. Their leader, a woman named Lyra Swiftarrow, was as skilled a strategist as she was a skilled archer, capable of launching arrows with deadly accuracy.

Lyra Swiftarrow, like Borin Stonehand, was initially skeptical. She was shrewd and observant, her eyes betraying a deep-seated distrust of outsiders. However, Elara's diplomacy, Finn's strategic insights, Falon's captivating stories, and Gerald's unexpected tactical analysis gradually won her over. Gerald's detailed analysis of Aldar's supply routes, and his ability to identify weak points in Aldar's defenses, deeply impressed Lyra.

Lyra, intrigued by their evident capabilities and their unwavering determination, agreed to join their cause. The River Folk would provide crucial support during the battle, utilizing their intimate knowledge of the marshes and waterways to launch surprise attacks and disrupt Aldar's logistics. Their skills in archery and ambush tactics would prove invaluable, providing a significant advantage in the upcoming battle.

With the Silver Peak warriors and the River Folk on their side, the alliance grew substantially stronger. The news of these two powerful clans joining their cause spread like wildfire across Coron, inspiring other smaller factions to rally to their banner. The initial fear and despair began to transform into a growing sense of hope and defiance. The momentum was turning. Aldar's seemingly unstoppable advance was now being challenged by the unity and determination of a kingdom awakened from its slumber. The battle ahead would still be dangerous, and the odds remained stacked against them, but now they were far from alone. They had gathered allies, forged alliances, and awakened a kingdom. The stage was set for a battle that would decide the fate of Coron. The time for achieving a victory was now closer than before.

The days that followed were a blur of intense training and preparation. The Sanctuary, usually a haven of quiet contemplation, transformed into a bustling hub of activity. The air hummed with the energy of focused determination, a harsh sense of urgency hanging heavily in the air. Elara, with her innate magical abilities, oversaw the enhancement of their physical capabilities. She devised a series of rigorous exercises designed to push their bodies and minds to their limits, honing their reflexes and strengthening their resolve.

Gerald, initially hesitant and unsure of his role, discovered a surprising aptitude for physical training. His determination, fueled by a newfound sense of responsibility and a growing understanding of the stakes involved, pushed him beyond his perceived limitations. He trained alongside Falon, learning the basics of swordsmanship from the spirited dwarf, her movements precise and deadly. Falon, in turn, was fascinated by Gerald's analytical mind, finding his strategic insights invaluable in refining her combat techniques. She taught him the nuances of dwarf crafted weaponry, the subtle art of utilizing traps and ambushes. Gerald's methodical approach complemented her instinctive warrior skills, creating a synergistic partnership.

Finn, the strategist focused on refining their battle tactics. He devised intricate battle plans, scenarios that considered every possible contingency. He engaged the group in war games, simulating various battle situations, pushing them to think strategically, to adapt to changing conditions, and to respond effectively under pressure. Finn's analytical mind and strategic expertise were invaluable in preparing them for the impending confrontation.

Elara, beyond her physical training, focused on enhancing their magical capabilities. She taught them basic defensive spells, shields of energy to protect against enemy attacks, and techniques for enhancing their senses, allowing them to perceive their surroundings more acutely. She emphasized the importance of harnessing their inner strength, to bolster their magical prowess. Gerald, surprised by his own latent abilities, found himself able to channel a small amount of magical energy, a surprising revelation that bolstered his confidence and resolve.

The training sessions were grueling. Day after day the relentless pace pushing them to their physical and mental limits. But the shared hardship forged a powerful bond amongst them. They learned to rely on each other, to trust in each other's abilities, and to anticipate each other's moves. The laughter and camaraderie that punctuated their training sessions lightened the burden of the impending battle, reminding them of the human element amidst the looming threat. They celebrated small victories and offered support during times of frustration and despair. They shared stories and anecdotes that provided respite from the weight of their mission.

Beyond the physical and magical training, they focused on preparing the supplies that were essential for their survival. Falon, meticulously checked and rechecked their equipment, ensuring that their weapons, armor, and supplies were in perfect order. She taught them how to improvise, how to create tools and weapons from readily available resources.

Gerald, surprisingly, contributed significantly to this phase of their preparation. His knowledge of practical problem solving, his ability to identify and address potential difficulties before they arose, surprised everyone. His analytical skills, previously limited to analyzing literary plots, now helped them anticipate the complexities of battle. He developed ingenious systems for managing resources and allocating supplies, ensuring that they remained well equipped throughout their campaign.

Evenings brought a different kind of preparation – mental fortification. They spent time discussing strategy, reviewing plans, and anticipating different scenarios. They studied maps, poring over details of the terrain, identifying potential chokepoints and defensive positions. They analyzed Aldar's tactics, recounting patterns and vulnerabilities that could be exploited. The mental preparations were as crucial as the physical ones.

The mental preparation also included bolstering their spirits. They shared stories of their past, personal struggles and victories, reinforcing the bonds of friendship and creating a stronger sense of unity. The support they provided each other, their mutual encouragement, proved as potent as any spell or sword.

As the day of the battle drew closer, a sense of quiet resolve settled over the Sanctuary. More rigorous training, the meticulous preparation, the forging of alliances – all these culminated in a sense of readiness. They were not just a group of warriors; they were a unified force, prepared to face any challenge, a coalition of talents ready to challenge the very essence of evil. There was an unspoken understanding that the future of Coron depended on in the Kingdom to be unified as one force. They had trained, they had prepared, and they were ready to fight for their lives, for their friends, and Coron.

The final days before the march to Aldar's fortress were punctuated by a strange, unsettling quietness. The frenetic energy of the previous weeks had subsided, replaced by a focused intensity. Each member of their unlikely fellowship seemed to be engaged in a private communion with their own thoughts, silent preparation for the battles to come. Even though Falon, usually a whirlwind of activity, seemed subdued, her usual boisterous laughter muted to a thoughtful silence.

For Gerald, this period was marked by a gradual awakening, a slow unfolding of the magical abilities he'd unknowingly acquired from the pool in the enchanted forest. Initially, the changes seemed small, almost imperceptible. He found he could concentrate more effectively, his mind sharper, his thoughts more focused. Simple tasks, like tracking the movement of birds in the forest or following the intricate patterns of a spider's web, felt easier, his senses enhanced with an almost supernatural acuity. The world around him seemed to become richer, more vibrant, woven with a thousand unseen threads of energy.

One evening, while meditating under Elara's guidance, Gerald felt warmth spread through his body, starting deep in his chest and radiating outward. It wasn't unpleasant, more like a gentle internal sun warming him from within. As the sensation intensified, he felt a tingle in his fingertips, a strange energy pulsing just beneath his skin. He instinctively raised his hand, and a faint, shimmering light emanated from his palm, a soft, fluctuating glow. He lowered his hand, startled, and the light disappeared as quickly as it had appeared.

Elara, observing him with a knowing smile, nodded slowly. "The pool...it has awakened something within you, Gerald. A dormant power, slumbering for centuries, perhaps longer."

Over the following days, Gerald's powers grew gradually stronger. He experimented with the light, finding he could control its intensity and duration to a limited extent. The light was not just a visual phenomenon; he discovered it held warmth that could soothe minor aches and pains. He tried projecting the light further, and while it still remained weak, he found that it held an unexpected potency; a small, withered plant in the Sanctuary garden sprang back to life when he focused the light upon it.

These nascent magical abilities weren't limited to light. He found he could manipulate small objects – a stray pebble would shift position slightly, or a fallen leaf would seem to dance gently on the breeze under the influence of his subtle control. He practiced these abilities in secret, mostly out of embarrassment. He was, after all, a writer, a man of words, not magic. Yet, the inherent power growing within him felt both fascinating and frightening.

His training with Elara focused on controlling this power, learning to channel it, to focus its intensity. She explained that his abilities were unique, not tied to the traditional schools of Coronian magic, but rather originating from some deeper, more ancient source. This was also confirmed by Finn, who recognized something fundamentally different about Gerald's magic. He suggested that Gerald's magic might be tied to the very nature of the interdimensional rift that had brought him to Coron, drawing its power from the raw, untamed energies of the multiverse.

Falon remained skeptical but supportive. She saw the potential benefit, viewing Gerald's powers as another weapon in their arsenal against Aldar. She even devised ingenious ways to incorporate his abilities into their battle strategies. She envisioned scenarios where Gerald could use his light to illuminate dark areas, provide distractions, or possibly even disable magical traps and wards placed by Aldar's sorcerers.

The training sessions continued, but with a new focus. Gerald worked to master his fledgling abilities, to merge them with the physical and strategic training. He discovered that focusing his magic enhanced his physical reflexes, making his movements faster, stronger, and more precise. He could channel his magic into his swordsmanship, imbuing his strikes with an extra surge of power. It was as if his magic wasn't merely an additional skill, but an integral part of him, a deepening of his very being.

His progress wasn't without its setbacks. There were times when the magic felt overwhelming, threatening to surge uncontrollably, causing him to lose focus or experience surges of intense dizziness. Elara carefully guided him through these moments, teaching him to breathe, to center himself, to ground his power within himself.

Beyond the physical exercises, Elara taught him techniques to bolster his mental defenses. Aldar and his sorcerers were skilled at manipulating minds, and Elara insisted that Gerald strengthen his own mental shield to protect himself from their influence. She taught him meditation techniques, visualization exercises, and ways to deflect psychic assaults.

Gerald felt a growing confidence in his abilities. He was no longer the hesitant writer who had stumbled into this world. He was a warrior, a mage, a vital part of the defense of Coron. His powers were still emerging, but he understood their potential. He understood his role. His understanding wasn't just about magical prowess; it was about a deeper understanding of himself, of the interwoven tapestry of destiny that had brought him here. He had become more than just a writer; he was becoming something more, something far greater than he could have ever imagined.

The night before the march, they gathered around a crackling fire, sharing stories, a silent acknowledgment of the perils that lay ahead. The usual jokes and banter felt subdued, replaced by a quiet solemnity. But there was no despair, only a deep, abiding sense of purpose. They looked at each other, not with fear, but with mutual respect and trust. They were ready, not just for the battle, but for whatever the future held. They were a team, forged in the crucible of war, strengthened by shared adversity, and empowered by an unlikely alliance between a writer and a world he never knew existed. And at the heart of that alliance stood Gerald, his newfound magical powers humming quietly beneath his skin, a silent testament to his extraordinary journey. The fate of Coron, it seemed, rested not only on their swords and spells, but on the quiet, unwavering determination of a writer who had found his destiny in the most unexpected of places.

The days leading up to the march were intense, while forging weapons were important, so were the bonds of comradery. Gerald, initially an outsider, a bewildered writer thrust into a world of magic and warfare, found himself inextricably woven into the fabric of their lives. He saw the genuine camaraderie, the unspoken understanding that transcended words. He witnessed the deep affection between Elara and Finn, bonded by years of shared responsibility and mutual respect. Their love for Coron was profound, a fierce, unwavering loyalty that fueled their determination.

Falon, initially wary of the "human," as she called him, had become a steadfast friend, a constant source of practical advice and boisterous encouragement. Her skepticism about Gerald's magic had softened into grudging admiration. She saw his dedication, the effort he put into mastering his abilities, the way he adapted his unique skills to their overall strategy. Her usual playful teasing was laced with genuine concern, a testament to the growing trust between them. She even shared some of her own personal stories, revealing vulnerabilities that hinted at a past hardship and a fierce loyalty to those she considered family.

Gerald, in turn, found himself deeply attached to them. He'd initially felt like an intruder, an accidental participant in a war far beyond his comprehension. But as he trained alongside them, as he shared their anxieties and hopes, he felt a growing sense of belonging. Their shared experiences in the Black Forest, their close calls with Aldar's scouts, had cemented a bond forged in shared danger and mutual reliance. He was no longer just Gerald Weaver, a writer; he was a member of their fellowship.

Their training became a ritual, a shared pilgrimage toward a common goal. They pushed each other, challenged each other, supported each other through moments of frustration and despair. Elara, with her serene wisdom, provided guidance, ensuring Gerald's powers were channeled effectively, preventing any uncontrolled bursts of energy. Finn, the stoic warrior and strategist, focused on physical combat, his training sessions with Gerald a practical demonstration of combining magic with physical prowess.

One training exercise involved a mock assault on a makeshift fortress constructed from fallen logs and branches. Gerald, using his light magic, illuminated hidden passages and illuminated weak points in the defenses while Falon used her dwarven ingenuity to create diversions. Finn, with his formidable swordsmanship, played the role of the attacking force, teaching Gerald to anticipate enemy movements and utilize his abilities for strategic advantage. Elara observed, offering insightful corrections and praise, her guidance subtle yet decisive. The exercise was more than just physical preparation; it was a symphony of combined strengths, a testament to their growing synergy.

Their bond wasn't just born out of shared danger and rigorous training. It was also cultivated through shared stories and laughter. Gerald shared anecdotes from his life as a writer, his struggles with writer's block, his triumphs and failures. He recounted his initial bewilderment upon arriving in Coron, the surrealism of his sudden displacement, and the gradual unfolding of his magical abilities. His stories, often laced with humor and self-deprecating wit, lightened the mood, helping them cope with the impending battle.

One evening, Falon recounted a tale of a daring heist she'd orchestrated as a young dwarf, her mischievous grin revealing a hint of pride and a touch of regret. Gerald found himself laughing, not only at the absurdity of the tale but also at her candid vulnerability. He saw in her a reflection of his own rebellious spirit, a willingness to break the rules to achieve a higher purpose.

Another evening, Elara shared a somber story about a past protector of the Sanctuary who had sacrificed themselves to save Coron from a similar threat. The story underscored the weight of their responsibility, the gravity of their mission, the price of protecting their kingdom. But even in the sadness of the story, there was a sense of shared determination, a resolute refusal to let past sacrifices be in vain.

Gerald expressed his desire to return to his world, yet he acknowledged the profound changes that had occurred within him. His experiences in Coron, his friendships, his newfound powers, were irrevocably changing him.

Falon spoke of rebuilding her family's workshop, which had been destroyed. Her dream wasn't just about restoring a physical structure; it was about preserving her dwarven heritage, her family's legacy. Finn, normally reticent about his personal life, shared his hope for a peaceful future for Coron, a future where the people could live without fear of invasion and tyranny.

They were no longer just a group of warriors preparing for a battle; they were a family, a fellowship forged in adversity, bound by shared experiences, strengthened by mutual trust and affection. It was a camaraderie born not just of necessity, but of genuine affection, a powerful force that would carry them through the darkness of the coming battle. The battle for Coron would be a test of their combined strength, but more importantly, their enduring power of friendship and unwavering loyalty.

6

The First Battles

The first rays of dawn painted the eastern sky in hues of
fiery orange and soft pink, a stark contrast to the grim anticipation that hung heavily in the air. An aura of tense silence hung in the atmosphere, broken only by the rustle of
leaves and the distant caw of a crow. For weeks, the Coronians had prepared, honing their skills, strengthening their
bonds, bracing themselves for the inevitable clash with Aldar's forces. Now, the moment had arrived.

The initial assault wasn't a full-scale invasion, not yet. It
was a probing assault, a calculated test of Coron's defenses,
a viper's strike designed to gauge their strength and identify
weaknesses. The attack began not with a thunderous roar of
charging armies, but with a subtle shift in the atmosphere,
a creeping unease that snaked through the ranks of the defenders.

Their strategy was clear: to sow chaos, to test the resilience of the Coronians, to disrupt their ranks before

launching an offensive. Coron's defenders, alerted by the advance scouts, reacted swiftly, their training kicking in instinctively. Elara, with her innate magical sensitivity, sensed the approach of the enemy long before they were visible, her eyes flashing with an inner light as she directed the placement of defensive enchantments. Finn, a whirlwind of motion, moved among the soldiers, his commanding presence inspiring confidence and order amidst the chaos. Falon, with her uncanny ability to anticipate enemy movements, directed the deployment of countermeasures, her sharp wit and quick thinking proved invaluable.

Gerald, armed with his newly discovered light magic, played a crucial role in coordinating the defense. He wasn't a seasoned warrior like Finn, nor a tactical genius like Falon, but he possessed a unique ability to see the battlefield in a way others could not. His light magic illuminated hidden areas, revealed the positions of enemy archers, and guided the movement of the defenders, allowing them to respond effectively to the enemy's unexpected maneuvers. He worked in concert with Elara, his light weaving through the defensive enchantments she placed, amplifying their power and extending their reach. His light magic also served as a a reassuring presence in the midst of the chaos, its luminous glow cutting through the gloom of the forest, bolstering the spirits of the defenders.

The initial volley of poisoned arrows caused some casualties, a grim reminder of the dangers they faced. The poison, unlike anything the Coronians had encountered before, slowing reflexes and dulling senses. Those struck by the arrows needed immediate attention, their wounds treated with potent antidotes prepared by Elara using rare herbs and magical concoctions. The battle wasn't just about brute force; it was a complex interplay of strategy, magic, and precise medical intervention.

The archers were followed by waves of foot soldiers, monstrous orcs and hulking goblins, their numbers far exceeding expectations. They pressed their attack against the perimeter, exploiting weaknesses in the defenses identified by the initial arrow barrage. The battle raged, a chaotic ballet of swords and spells, of screams and cries, of courage and desperation. Finn, leading the charge, fought with the ferocity of a cornered lion, his sword a blur of motion, slicing through the enemy ranks. Falon, using her ingenuity, created ingenious traps and diversions, slowing the enemy's advance. The battle raged for hours, the sounds of clashing steel and magical explosions echoing through the forest. Gerald, though initially overwhelmed by the chaos and violence, quickly adapted, his magic became more precise, and he learned to focus his light magic, not just to illuminate the battlefield, but also to create blinding flashes, disorienting the enemy and giving the Coronian soldiers a crucial advantage. He learned to channel his light into protective shields, deflecting enemy blows and shielding his comrades. The magic enhance their weapons, making their swords strike with greater force, their arrows fly with greater accuracy.

The battle was not without its losses. Brave Coronians fell, in sacrifice to their unwavering loyalty to their kingdom. Gerald witnessed firsthand the horrors of war, the pain and suffering it inflicted. But he also witnessed the resilience of the Coronians, their determination to protect their homes and loved ones. Their unity, forged in the crucible of battle, was a sight to behold. The bond they had built during their training wasn't just a matter of words; it was a tangible force that carried them through the brutal fight.

As the sun began to set, casting long shadows across the battlefield, the initial assault began to wane. Aldar's forces, having failed to breach Coron's defenses, retreated into the Black Forest, leaving behind a trail of death and destruction. The victory was hard-won, but a victory, nonetheless. The initial test had been passed. Coron stood firm.

The immediate aftermath of the battle was a scene of both triumph and tragedy. The wounded were tended to, their injuries treated with the utmost care. The fallen were mourned, their memory honored with respect and solemn rituals. Gerald, despite his growing magical proficiency, felt the weight of the losses deeply, the reality of death in this world striking him with a profound sorrow. He saw Elara's face filled sadness as she worked tirelessly to tend the wounded, and Finn's quiet intensity as he surveyed the battlefield, his face a mask of grim determination. Falon's usually cheerful face was solemn. The experience had marked him, had stripped away any lingering illusions of this being just another fantasy. This was real, with real consequences.

But amidst the sorrow, there was also a sense of pride and camaraderie. They had faced Aldar's initial assault and prevailed. The bond between them had been tested in the fires of battle and emerged stronger, more profound than ever before. They had proven their strength, their unity, their resilience. The first battle was over, but the war was far from finished. The coming battles promised to be even more fierce and demanding, and the Coronians would need all their courage, all their skill, and above all, their unity if they were to survive. The victory had come at a cost; they would face the coming darkness together.

The settling sound fell over the battlefield. The fields on fire, dark clouds loomed with the scent of blood and woodsmoke, a tangible echo of the clash of steel. Gerald, despite the exhaustion, found himself strangely exhilarated. The raw, visceral experience of combat, the adrenaline-fueled dance between life and death, had forged something within him – a newfound confidence, a sharper awareness of his own capabilities.

His light magic, initially tentative and uncertain, had blossomed under the pressure of battle. He'd learned to weave his light into intricate patterns, creating shimmering shields that deflected blows, blinding flashes that disoriented the enemy, and concentrated beams that amplified the Coronians' weapons. He'd witnessed firsthand how his seemingly insignificant abilities had helped tipped the scales of battle.

His role hadn't been limited to offensive magic. He had discovered the subtle art of defensive light weaving, creating shimmering veils that deflected arrows and absorbed the impact of blows. He had become not just a fighter, a protector, an integral part of the Coronian defense. His understanding of the battlefield had also evolved. He'd discovered an almost precognitive ability to anticipate enemy movements, his light instinctively guiding him to positions of strategic importance. He could sense the flow of battle, the ebb and flow of energy, the subtle shifts in momentum. He learned to recognize the telltale signs of enemy ambushes and countermeasures, using his light magic to alert his comrades and neutralize the threat. It wasn't just a tool he wielded; it was a part of him, a reflection of his own spirit, his own strength.

The aftermath of the battle revealed the true cost of their victory. The Sanctuary, usually a haven of peace and tranquility, was transformed into a field hospital. Elara worked tirelessly, she guided the wounded to different areas depending on their injuries.. Finn, his normally boisterous spirit subdued, moved among the injured, offering words of comfort and support. Falon, though visibly shaken by the violence, displayed an incredible resilience, assisting Elara with her healing tasks. The air was thick with the scent of herbs and magical concoctions, a testament to Elara's skill and dedication.

Gerald found himself drawn to the wounded. He worked alongside Elara, learning from her vast knowledge of herbal remedies and magical healing techniques. He discovered a surprising affinity for this aspect of his new role, finding a strange solace in alleviating the suffering of others. It was a different kind of combat, a battle fought not with swords and spells, but with compassion and healing energy. Aldar wasn't just a conqueror; he was a force of darkness, a symbol of despair, a threat to the very fabric of existence.

The next few days were spent in preparation for the inevitable second assault. The wounds of the first battle were still raw, but the Coronians showed no signs of wavering. Their determination had been tempered in the crucible of combat, forged into an unbreakable resolve. Their honed skills and strengthened defenses, they were ready for whatever Aldar might throw at them.

Gerald, his confidence bolstered by his performance in the first battle, took a more active role in strategic planning. He shared his unique insights into Aldar's tactics; his observations gleaned from his light enhanced vision of the battlefield. He proposed new defensive strategies, utilizing

his understanding to anticipate enemy movements. His suggestions, initially met with some skepticism, were quickly accepted as his predictions proved remarkably accurate. His unique perspective had become an invaluable asset to the Coronians.

He continued to polish his magical skills, experimenting with new techniques and refining existing ones. He discovered that his light magic could be used not only for combat and healing, but also for communication and reconnaissance. He learned to use his light to create illusions, to mask the movements of his comrades and deceive the enemy. His abilities were evolving at an astonishing rate empowered by his growing understanding of his own potential.

The days turned into weeks; each filled with anticipation and preparation. The Coronians, united by their shared purpose and their deep-seated resilience, waited for the next onslaught. The quiet before the storm was far more tense than the chaos of the first battle; the unmistakable sense of foreboding lingered in the air. Gerald, along with the other defenders, knew that the next battle would be even more difficult, more brutal, and more decisive. But they were ready. They had faced the darkness once and emerged victorious. They were ready to bear that continued weight. The coming battles would test them to their limits, but their unity, forged in the fires of the first battle, would be a shining light in the darkest hours.

A hollowing war cry ripped through the air, a guttural roar that pulsated down Gerald's spine despite his growing familiarity with the sounds of battle. The second assault was underway, even more ferocious than the first. Aldar's forces, bolstered by fresh reinforcements, surged forward like a tide of black, their numbers seemingly endless. Arrows rained down like deadly hail, and the clash of steel echoed through the forest, a deafening symphony of destruction.

Gerald, his light weaving a shimmering shield around him, fought alongside the Coronians, his magic a beacon of hope in the swirling chaos. He saw Elara, her face resolute, directing the defenders with unwavering efficiency, her own magic, a tempest of wind and fire. Finn, fought with immense strength, his axe cleaving through enemy ranks. But it was Falon, the young female dwarf, who truly captured Gerald's attention.

Her size, which initially seemed a disadvantage, had become her greatest strength. She moved with a speed and agility that belied her stature, darting through the fray like a whirlwind of destruction. Her axe, surprisingly light yet devastatingly powerful, danced with deadly grace, leaving a trail of fallen enemies in its wake. She was a blur of motion, a force of nature unleashed, her every strike precise and deadly.

Gerald watched, awestruck, as she faced down a towering ogre, its club the size of a small tree. The ogre roared, its breath a fetid cloud that threatened to overwhelm Falon, but she didn't flinch. With a defiant cry, she launched herself at the beast, her axe flashing in the dim light of the forest. She dodged the clumsy swipe of the ogre's club. She danced around the creature, a miniature warrior facing a colossal foe, her attacks relentless and accurate.

She didn't rely solely on brute strength. Gerald noted her cunning strategy. Instead of a direct confrontation, she used the ogre's own bulk against it, luring it closer to a tangle of thick tree roots. As the ogre stumbled, she expertly took advantage of the momentary loss of balance, delivering a precise blow to its ankle joint. The ogre collapsed under its own weight, its roar turning into a pained groan.

But the battle was far from over. Another threat emerged from the shadows – Morack, Aldar's master sorcerer. His magic, dark and twisted, crackled with fierce energy, weaving spells of shadow and death. He moved with unnerving speed, his spells striking with terrifying precision, leaving a trail of fallen Coronians in his wake.

Seeing the danger, Falon moved with a speed that bordered on impossible. Despite the chaos of battle, she saw an opening, a gap in Morack's defenses. She did not hesitate. She charged, her axe held high, a tiny but fierce figure rushing toward the powerful sorcerer. Morack, seemingly surprised by her audacity, raised his hands to deflect her attack. However, Falon anticipated this, altering her trajectory at the last moment. She slipped past his defenses, striking at his side with unexpected precision. The blow wasn't fatal, but it was enough to break Morack's concentration, disrupting his flow of magic, disorienting Morack and giving the Coronians the time they needed to regroup and counterattack. Falon, not wasting the chance, leveraged the confusion and delivered another powerful blow, knocking Morack to the ground.

The brief respite, bought with Falon's courage and tactical genius, was crucial. The Coronians, rejuvenated by their unexpected success, continued the assault. The tide of the battle began to shift. Morack, though still a formidable opponent, was visibly shaken, his power hampered by Falon's unexpected bravery.

However, the victory was far from assured. The battle raged on, each moment a desperate struggle for survival. Finn continued to bolster the defenses of the Coronians. He observed Falon's tactical brilliance, marveling at her ability to anticipate enemy movements and exploit their weaknesses.

As the battle reached its climax, Falon found herself face to face with a monstrous, heavily armored knight – one of Aldar's most elite warriors. The knight's armor gleamed darkly, reflecting the flickering light of the battle. Its weapon, a massive Warhammer, crackled with dark magic. The sheer size and power of the knight were intimidating, but Falon showed no fear. She met the knight's gaze, her own eyes blazing with determination.

This duel was a stark contrast to the chaotic melee surrounding them. It was a dance of death, a precise and deadly ballet between the two warriors. The knight swung its Warhammer with brutal force, the blows shattering trees and tearing at the earth. But Falon, quick and agile, evaded each strike with speed and agility. She moved like a shadow, her axe flashing out like a streak of lightning, finding weak points in the knight's armor. The fight with the Knight was a true test of skills and courage. She wasn't just fighting for survival; it was a fight for a Kingdom and the downfall of Aldar's tyranny. With a final, desperate lunge, she managed to deliver a decisive blow. Her axe, guided by precision and willpower, pierced a gap in the knight's armor, reaching its vital organs. The armored knight crashed to the ground; its body lay lifeless.

As the dust settled, and the echoes of battle began to fade, it became clear that the Coronians had achieved a hard fought victory. But the cost had been steep. The ground was littered with the bodies of fallen comrades. The air was still filled with the stench of blood and burnt magic. Yet, amidst the carnage, a renewed sense of hope had taken root. They had won the second battle. The Coronians had faced the might of Aldar's forces and had repelled them for now. Their battles would be etched in the annals of Coron's history, alongside Gerald's unlikely emergence as a Bridgebinder, a warrior of light amidst the encroaching darkness. The triumph, while hard-earned, had instilled a sense of resolve within the hearts of the Coronians. They knew there were more battles to come, but they also knew, now more than ever, that they possessed the strength, the courage, and the unity to face Aldar's relentless attacks. The weary defenders of Coron, now united by their shared ordeal and victory, turned their attention towards the painstaking task once again of healing the wounded and preparing, knowing that this was not the end but merely a pivotal moment in the epic conflict for the future of their kingdom.

The initial euphoria of their victory began to fade as the sun dipped below the horizon, casting long shadows across the ravaged battlefield carried the mournful cries of the wounded. Their celebratory mood was muted, replaced by a sobering assessment of the cost of their triumph. Many brave Coronians lay still, their sacrifices a stark reminder of the brutal reality of battle.

Elara, filled with exhaustion but her eyes unwavering, oversaw the tending of more wounded. The strain on Elara's magic, usually a tempest of vibrant energy, now flowed with a quiet intensity, healing wounds and soothing fractured spirits. Finn, solemnly moved through the fallen, his face blank from expression as he paid his respects to those who had given their lives.

Gerald, still adjusting to his role, found himself strangely comforted by the shared grief and exhaustion. The camaraderie forged in the heat of battle had created a bond that transcended their different origins.

He saw how the Coronians supported each other, sharing what little food and water they had left, comforting the grieving, and tending to the injured with a dedication that spoke volumes about their resilience and strength. The Coronians, despite their exhaustion, worked tirelessly to clear the battlefield, burying their fallen comrades with the respect and dignity they deserved. They gathered what remained of their weapons and supplies, assessing their losses and planning for the battles to come. The logistical challenges were immense; the supply lines were stretched thin, and resources were scarce. But their spirits, though weary, were far from broken. Small strategic victories had instilled a sense of newfound confidence, a belief that they could stand against Aldar's might.

The first strategic victory after the initial battle was a daring raid on one of Aldar's outlying supply depots. Information gathered from captured prisoners revealed the location of a crucial stockpile of weapons and supplies, located in a seemingly impenetrable fortress nestled deep within a treacherous mountain pass. Elara, using her knowledge and her ability to manipulate the winds, devised a plan to infiltrate the storage supply under the cover of a ferocious blizzard. The blizzard, carefully orchestrated by Elara, obscured their movements from Aldar's scouts, allowing them to approach the fortress undetected.

Falon, her agility and knowledge of stealth tactics invaluable, led the small contingent of Coronians through the treacherous mountain pass. They navigated the blizzard with the skill of seasoned mountain climbers, their movements fluid and silent. They avoided Aldar's patrols, utilizing the swirling snow as camouflage. Gerald, his light magic providing illumination and guidance in the blinding snow.

The assault on the depot was swift and brutal. The element of surprise, coupled with the Coronians' fierce determination, caught Aldar's minions off guard. They stormed the depot, overwhelming the outnumbered and unprepared orcs. The raid was a resounding success, resulting in the seizure of a significant cache of weapons and supplies that would greatly strengthen Coron's defenses. The victory was celebrated a knowing that every resource they secured was another step closer to a possiblity winning the final battle.

Their next strategic triumph involved disrupting Aldar's supply lines. Gerald, using his newfound magical abilities, discovered a pattern in Aldar's movements; his forces relied on a network of hidden tunnels and subterranean passages to transport supplies and reinforcements. By identifying these weak points, the Coronians were able to launch a series of targeted strikes, destroying key sections of these tunnels, thus disrupting Aldar's ability to resupply his forces effectively. The effect was devastating. Aldar's army, already strained by previous defeats, was now increasingly hampered by supply shortages.

These strategic victories were not achieved without further losses. Each encounter with Aldar's forces resulted in some casualties, reminding the Coronians of the constant risk. Each successful strike boosted morale and strengthened the Coronian fighters resolve. The strategic approach, by weakening Aldar's strength rather than direct confrontation, proved remarkably effective.

Aldar's forces, once an unstoppable tide, were now increasingly hampered by logistical problems and dwindling morale. The Coronians, though battered and bruised, had proven their capacity to adapt and outmaneuver their formidable enemy. The small but effective attacks sowed seeds of hope and resilience within the kingdom. They showcased not only their courage, but also their tactical acumen and their ability to utilize their unique skills and resources effectively.

News of Coron's unexpected victories against Aldar's seemingly invincible army began to spread beyond the kingdom's borders. Whispers of the courageous Coronians, led by their remarkable dwarf warrior, and aided by the mysterious newcomer from another world, reached even the ears of those who had been conquered by Aldar. These small campaigns, born from a combination of courage, strategy, and unlikely alliances, sparked a flicker of hope in the hearts of those who had long suffered under Aldar's oppressive rule. It became a beacon of defiance. And as the whispers turned into rumors, and the rumors into a burgeoning rebellion, Gerald and the Coronians knew future successes may lead to one major victory for the Kingdom of Coron. The future was still uncertain, but the narrative was shifting, the balance of power offered a glimmer of hope in the looming uncertainty. The tide of battle was changing.

The celebratory bonfires crackled, casting flickering shadows on the faces of the weary warriors. But the warmth of the flames couldn't entirely dispel the chill that settled among Coron, a creeping chill from the lingering night air, and the grim reality of their losses.

Amongst the fallen lay Captain Theron, his broad chest pierced by a sorcerer's bolt, his usually booming laughter silenced forever. Theron, a veteran of countless battles, had been a pillar of strength, his unwavering courage inspiring his men. His loss left a gaping hole in the Coronian ranks, a void that would be difficult to fill. Beside him, young Elara knelt, her face, a mask of sorrow as she gently closed his eyes, a silent farewell to a comrade and a friend. Tears streamed down her usually stoic face, blurring the lines etched by exhaustion. The weight of her grief was enormous, a heavy blanket smothering the tentative joy of their triumph.

Further down the field, amidst the scattered remnants of weapons and broken shields, lay Jude, one of the kingdom's renowned archers. His accuracy was legendary, his arrows finding their mark with deadly precision. But even his skill couldn't deflect the onslaught of Aldar's forces. A stray bolt of dark magic had struck him, silencing his deadly aim permanently. His death was a profound loss, not just for his exceptional skill, but for his spirit and infectious optimism. Jude had been a source of encouragement, a hope in the darkest moments, and his absence would be acutely felt.

The losses extended beyond the immediate battlefield. News trickled in from outlying villages, tales of skirmishes and ambushes, of brave Coronian fighters falling to Aldar's relentless advance. Each report brought with it a new wave of grief, a fresh reminder of the cost of this war. The whispers of these losses snaked through the camp, weaving a tapestry of sorrow that threatened to overshadow their victory. The faces of the survivors reflected the collective mourning; each face with the pain of loss and the apprehension of what lay ahead.

Even Finn seemed affected. He moved among the wounded, his strong hands tending to injuries with practiced ease, but his eyes held a deep well of sorrow that no amount of outward bravado could mask. The battle had tested their resilience and taken a heavy toll on their spirits.

The next few days were a blur of grim activity. The burial pyres burned continuously, casting an eerie orange glow against the night sky. The air was filled with the mournful chants of the priests, their voices a somber chorus echoing the collective sorrow of the kingdom. The ground was freshly turned, each mound of earth a silent testament to the sacrifices made.

Gerald, witnessing this heartbreaking ritual, felt a profound sense of loss, a deep connection to the pain of these people he had only recently come to know. He had not known these individuals personally, yet their deaths felt like a personal tragedy. The shared grief transcended cultural and temporal boundaries, forging a bond between him and the Coronians that was as strong as any he had ever experienced. He had been an outsider, a stranger thrust into a world he barely understood, yet he felt inexplicably bound to these people, their fates intertwined with his own.

The battle had depleted their resources, leaving them with a dire shortage of food, water, and medical supplies. The wounded cried out for healing, their pleas a constant reminder of the ongoing struggle. Elara, despite her exhaustion, worked tirelessly, her magic a lifeline sustaining the hope of many. But even her powerful magic could not reach everyone; the sheer number of injuries far exceeded the capacity of even the most gifted healers.

The aftermath of the battle forced a sobering reflection on their strategies. Their initial triumph had been exhilarating, but the price was devastating. It was a harsh lesson, a painful reminder that victory, even a decisive one, often came with unbearable losses. Every fallen warrior represented a broken family, a shattered community, a future stolen.

The quiet days following the battle were filled with a stoic determination. The kingdom was mourning, yes, but also regrouping, preparing for the inevitable next wave of Aldar's attacks. They buried their dead, tended their wounded, and steeled themselves for the battles ahead. The cost was high, but the spirit of Coron, battered but not broken, remained indomitable. The memories of the fallen served not as a deterrent, but as a powerful fuel, igniting a fiercer resolve to defend their kingdom, their families, and their futures.

The sense of unity forged in the crucible of battle became even stronger. They understood the fragility of life and the strength that came from collective grief and shared resolve.

They were united not only by their common cause, but by the shared experience of loss. The stories of the fallen became a reminder of their sacrifices and a testament to their courage, strengthening the bond between the survivors.

The battle had left deep scars, both physical and emotional. Yet, amongst the mourning, there was a growing understanding: they had bought themselves time. They had won a battle, but the war was far from over. The long road ahead remained treacherous, filled with uncertainty and danger. But the Coronians, inspired by the memory of their fallen comrades, were ready to face whatever Aldar threw at them. Their resolve, tempered by the fire of loss, burned brighter than ever before. They would fight, not just for survival, but for the legacy of those who had given their all for Coron. They would fight for the hope of a future free from Aldar's tyrannical grip, a future worth fighting for, even if it meant more sacrifices lay ahead.

7

The Siege of Coron

The days that followed were a grim procession of mounting tension. The initial elation of their hard-fought victory had evaporated, replaced by a sense of dread. The celebrations had been brief, quickly overshadowed by the stark reality of their losses and the looming threat that still hung heavy in the air. Aldar, far from being defeated, had merely retreated, regrouping his forces for a far more devastating assault.

The first sign was the absence of scouting parties. For days, the usual patrols that kept watch on the borders remained absent. Whispers spread through the city, carried on the wind like ominous premonitions. The silence was deafening, a stark contrast to the usual bustle of a kingdom preparing for war. Then came the sightings—isolated at first, then increasingly frequent—of Aldar's black banners snaking across the horizon, a creeping darkness that slowly enveloped Coron. The encirclement wasn't a swift, brutal strike. It was a slow, deliberate squeeze, a tightening noose that gradually choked the life out of the kingdom. Aldar's forces didn't rush headlong into another pitched battle. Instead, they established a perimeter, cutting off Coron's supply lines, isolating it from the rest of the world. Small bands of soldiers harassed the outlying villages, cutting off communication and disrupting any attempts at reinforcement.

The once vibrant markets fell silent. The streets, previously bustling with life, now echoed with an unnatural quiet, punctuated only by the anxious whispers of the citizenry. Food supplies dwindled, water sources were contaminated by Aldar's sorcerer Morack, and the constant threat of attack kept the populace in a state of perpetual fear. The initial courage and resolve from their previous victories began to fray at the edges, replaced by gnawing uncertainty.

Gerald, witnessing this slow strangulation of his adopted home, felt a rising tide of anger and frustration. His initial naivete about the complexities of warfare had been shattered. He had seen the brutal reality of battle firsthand, the horrifying cost of victory and the even more terrifying prospect of defeat. The jovial camaraderie of the Sanctuary felt like a distant memory, replaced by the harsh realities of siege warfare.

Elara tried to maintain order and morale, her magic working overtime to heal more wounded. But even her power had its limits. The constant drain on her energy was evident, the vibrant glow in her eyes dimmed by exhaustion and worry. She was a wellspring of hope for the Coronians, but even her light was beginning to flicker under the weight of the siege.

Finn, his usual canny manner subdued, took on the role of a tireless organizer. He oversaw the rationing of dwindling supplies, ensured that the defenses were maintained, and coordinated the city's limited resources. His leadership was crucial, a steadying influence amidst the growing chaos. But even his firm resolve couldn't completely mask the deep lines of worry engrained on his face. Falon worked tirelessly, her small frame a whirlwind of activity. She organized the women and children into teams, assigning tasks that made the best use of their limited skills. She oversaw the production of makeshift weapons, the strengthening of fortifications, and the rationing of any remaining food and supplies. Her efforts were crucial, keeping the morale of the civilians high amidst the despair and distress. Her spirit, however, showed signs of disquiet for the impending war.

The siege was not only a physical one, but a psychological one as well. Aldar's forces employed a range of tactics designed to break the Coronians' spirit. False promises of surrender, rumors of betrayal, and the constant bombardment of psychological warfare wore down the on the city's inhabitants. Sleep became a luxury, the constant fear like a heavy blanket smothering their confidence.

Nights were the hardest. The city was plunged into darkness, save for the flickering torches that cast long, dancing shadows on the anxious faces of its citizens. The sound of Aldar's forces moving around the city walls was a constant, unsettling reminder of their vulnerability. The occasional catapulted stones crashed into the walls, sending up plumes of dust and debris, a chilling demonstration of Aldar's might.

Days were barely better. The sky was perpetually overcast, mirroring the mood of the besieged city. The lack of sunlight made the city feel even colder, darker, and more oppressive. The stench of fear and decay, a suffocating blend that was further weighing the spirit of the Coronians.

The situation became critical as provisions dwindled to a mere fraction of what was needed. Hunger became a pervasive companion, gnawing at the bellies and eroding the spirit of the population. Disease spread quickly through the weakened populace, claiming lives at an alarming rate.

Despite the dire circumstances, the spirit of Coron remained unbroken. The people, battered and bruised, still clung to their hope, their determination fueled by their collective resolve and the belief in a better tomorrow. They rallied around their leaders, their faith strengthened by their mutual adversity.

Gerald, watching the Coronians endure, felt an overwhelming sense of admiration and respect. He had initially been a reluctant participant in this struggle, a bystander thrust into the heart of a conflict he hadn't chosen. But as the siege stretched on. He would fight alongside the Coronians, not just for survival, but for the preservation of a kingdom that had become his unexpected home. The siege was a test of endurance, An ordeal that would shape the futures of the kingdom and himself. The encirclement of Coron was complete, but the spirit of Coron refused to be broken. The battle for Coron had entered a new, far more protracted phase.

The dwindling supplies became a constant, gnawing worry. Finn, with his meticulous nature, helped with rigorous rationing system, ensuring that every morsel of food was distributed fairly. Hunger became a pervasive companion, gnawing at the bellies and eroding the spirit of the population. Disease spread quickly through the weakened populace, claiming lives at an alarming rate. But even his painstaking planning couldn't stave off the creeping hunger that began to plague the city. The once plump loaves of bread, baked fresh each morning in the city's ovens, had shrunk to meager portions, their crusts harder than stone. The rich stews, once brimming with hearty vegetables and succulent meats, were now thin watery broths, barely concealing their scarcity.

The children were the first to suffer. Their small frames, already frail from the constant stress and lack of sleep, were now weakened further by malnutrition. Their eyes, once bright and full of life, were now dull and listless, reflecting the bleak reality of their situation. Falon established makeshift nurseries within the city walls, offering the children what little comfort and nourishment she could. She sang them lullabies to soothe their fears, telling them tales of bravery and resilience to keep their spirits up, even as her own heart ached with worry.

The faces of the adults' once jovial and friendly were now gaunt and drawn, with the lines of exhaustion and hunger. Their energy levels had plummeted, making it increasingly difficult for them to perform even the most basic tasks. The city's defenses, once scrupulously maintained, began to show signs of neglect. The walls, weakened by the constant bombardment, developed cracks and fissures. The watchtowers, once manned with alert soldiers, were now sparsely guarded, the soldiers too weak to stand vigilant watch for long periods.

The lack of water became an even more pressing concern. Aldar's sorcerers, with their mastery of dark magic, had poisoned many of the city's water sources. The few remaining clean water sources were guarded jealously, precious droplets dispensed with caution and care. The once clear streams that flowed through the city were now stagnant and foul smelling, their waters unfit for human consumption. People lined up for hours, their parched throats begging for a meager sip of the precious liquid.

The relentless siege began to take its toll on the city's morale. The initial resolve that had characterized Coron's defense was gradually eroded by the weight of despair and hopelessness. The constant threat of attack, the ever-present hunger, and the pervasive fear created an ominous air of dread and foreboding. Rumors and whispers circulated through the city, spreading like wildfire and feeding the growing sense of panic. Some spoke of treason within the city's walls, others of Aldar's unstoppable might. Creeping whispers of despair were a subtle but powerful weapon in Aldar's arsenal, slowly chipping away at the resilience of the Coronians.

Gerald, witnessing the slow disintegration of the city's spirit, knew that something drastic had to be done. He couldn't just stand by and watch as Coron succumbed to despair. He was a writer, a storyteller, a weaver of words, and he realized that his skills, too, could be weapons in this battle. His words resonated with the people, striking a chord with their hearts and igniting a spark of hope in their despondent souls.

Gerald spoke of tools of resistance, designed to counter Aldar's propaganda. He spoke of Coron's glorious past, reminding them of their ancestors' bravery and their triumphs over adversity. He emphasized the importance of their collective strength and their shared destiny, emphasizing the critical need for unity and perseverance in the face of overwhelming odds. He shared anecdotes of bravery and sacrifice, inspiring them to continue the fight, not just for survival but for the preservation of their beloved city.

He also turned to Elara, seeking her help to counter Aldar's magical attacks. Elara, despite her exhaustion, eagerly embraced the challenge. Together, they devised a plan to create a protective magical barrier around the city's main water sources. The ritual was long and arduous, exhausting both their energies, but it was successful, creating a magical shield that protected the water from Aldar's dark spells. The small victory, however, came at a steep price; Elara's strength was dangerously depleted.

Finn, meanwhile, found himself dealing with the critical shortage of weapons and ammunition. The city's armory, once well stocked, was now almost empty. He scoured the city for any remaining weapons, organizing the citizens into teams to repair and refurbish whatever they could find. He encouraged Coronians to create makeshift weapons from everyday objects, turning farm tools and kitchen implements into crude but effective weapons. He tirelessly worked to maintain the city's defenses, even as his own strength faltered.

Falon took on another role in organizing the medical supplies for the city's wounded and sick. With her knowledge of herbal remedies, she created healing potions and ointments from the limited herbs and plants are still available within the city walls. She worked deligently, day and night to stockpile what they would need.

As the siege intensified, the kingdom found itself fighting on multiple fronts. Not only were they defending their city walls against Aldar's forces, but they were also battling hunger, disease, and the insidious erosion of their morale. The city was weakening, but its spirit, ignited by Gerald's words and fueled by the collective strength of its people, remained unyielding. The end of the siege was not in sight, but the people of Coron, spurred by the unlikely hero from another world, found strength in their adversity and continued their fight, clinging fiercely to their hope for a peaceful and prosperous kingdom.

The flickering lamplight cast long shadows across the cobbled alleyway as Elara, Finn, Falon, and Gerald huddled together, their faces grimacing with worry and determination. The siege had pushed Coron to its limits; the official defenses were crumbling, and despair threatened to consume the city. But in the shadowed corners, a different kind of resistance was brewing. A propaganda campaign, initially begun by a few courageous citizens, had blossomed into a network of clandestine cells, working in the shadows to undermine Aldar's grip on Coron.

This wasn't a formal army; it was a patchwork of individuals – artisans, merchants, scholars, even former soldiers too injured or elderly to fight on the walls. Their weapons were not swords and bows, but ingenuity and courage. They were the city's silent guardians, working secretly to disrupt Aldar's supply lines, spread rumors to sow dissent among his ranks, and to keep the flickering flame of hope alive in the hearts of the Coronians.

Their leader, a wizened old woman named Shaya, whose age belied a sharp mind and unwavering determination, had orchestrated this underground network with remarkable skill. Shaya, a former librarian, possessed an encyclopedic knowledge of Coron's history and its secret passages, a network of hidden tunnels and forgotten cellars that crisscrossed beneath the city. These were their pathways, their sanctuaries, and their arteries of resistance.

One of Shaya's most effective strategies was the spread of disinformation. She and her team of nimble-fingered scribes created forged documents, orders, and maps, designed to sow confusion and discord within Aldar's ranks. Fake orders detailing troop movements, false inventories of supplies, and even fabricated prophecies predicting Aldar's downfall were subtly slipped into the enemy camps, creating chaos and mistrust among the invaders.

Meanwhile, the artisans of the resistance had crafted a series of ingenious devices. Small, self-activating catapults, hidden in the city's sewers, launched bags of noxious herbs and stinging nettles into Aldar's camps, disrupting their routines and causing minor but persistent irritations. They also developed a network of hidden communication tunnels, allowing information to flow freely beneath the city, bypassing Aldar's patrols and spies.

Gerald, with his storytelling skills, became a crucial part of the resistance's propaganda efforts. He crafted stirring ballads and short, powerful poems, using his stories to reinforce hope and determination. These poems, passed from hand to hand, spoke of courage and defiance, of Coron's unwavering spirit and the inevitability of Aldar's defeat. His words, whispered in the shadowed corners of the city, fueled the embers of defiance, reminding the citizens of their heritage and their resilience.

Falon, with her knowledge of herbs and remedies, proved invaluable. She trained members of the resistance in the use of medicinal plants to treat injuries sustained during clandestine operations. She also developed potent sleeping draughts, used to incapacitate Aldar's guards and secure critical supplies. The sleeping draught, a carefully crafted mixture of moonflower, nightshade, and mandrake root, worked with surprising effectiveness.

Finn helped to map out the resistance networks, carefully detailing all their escape routes, communication channels, and caches of weapons and medical supplies. He had also devised a complex system of coded messages, ensuring that their communications were safe from interception. His expertise in logistics proved crucial, ensuring the smooth running of their clandestine activities.

Elara, though weakened from the previous magical exertions, continued to support the resistance with her magical abilities. She created small, enchanted charms, worn by the fighters of the resistance to protect them from Aldar's dark magic. These charms, woven with threads of moonlight and imbued with protective spells, offered a degree of resilience against Aldar's sorcery. They were small acts of defiance, potent symbols of resistance against the encroaching darkness. But the underground resistance was not without its risks. Aldar's spies were everywhere, their eyes and ears penetrating even the deepest recesses of the city. Several members of the resistance were captured, their fate uncertain. Yet, each time a member was lost, two more stepped forward to take their place. The spirit of Coron, though battered, refused to be broken.

One daring operation saw a small group of resistance fighters, led by Shaya, infiltrate Aldar's main supply depot located just outside the city walls. Disguised as Aldar's own troops, they managed to sabotage several critical supplies, including siege weapons and food rations. The operation was fraught with peril, but their success dealt a significant blow to Aldar's war effort.

Another covert operation involved the liberation of several Coronian prisoners held captive by Aldar's forces. A daring raid, cunningly planned by Finn, resulted in the release of a considerable number of prisoners, boosting morale significantly within the city and providing desperately needed reinforcements to the depleted Coronians' ranks.

As the siege continued, the activities of the underground resistance became increasingly audacious. Their acts of sabotage, coupled with Gerald's inspiring messages and Falon's medical ingenuity, created a sense of defiance that permeated Coron. The relentless efforts of Shaya and her followers instilled a belief that even under siege, there was still hope. The people of Coron, drawing strength from their clandestine allies, were more than just survivors; they were fighters, and they would not surrender. Their underground resistance, a silent symphony of courage and defiance, played a crucial role in shaping the course of the battle for Coron. Their spirit, though small against the darkness, would not be put out. The siege was a test of wills, a struggle between hope and despair, and the underground resistance played a critical role in tilting the balance towards hope. A silent revolution in the city's shadows gave it the strength to endure.

The flickering candlelight in Shaya's hidden chamber cast dancing shadows on Gerald's face. He sat hunched over a roughhewn table, his fingers tracing the worn lines of a tattered map of Coron. The constant rumble of Aldar's catapults a grim soundtrack to their desperate struggle. Yet, in this subterranean haven, a different kind of war was being waged – a war of whispers, shadows, and unwavering perseverance.

Gerald, initially a bewildered outsider, had rapidly become a central figure in the resistance. His unexpected journey from a writer's desk to the besieged city of Coron had given way to a burning resolve, fueled by a deep empathy for the Coronians and a growing understanding of his own unexpected role in their destiny.

Gerald's stories became a pulse for the resistance, mirroring their struggles, voicing their fears, and inspiring them to act. By revising old legends for present circumstances, he reinforced their belief that hope endures even in the darkest times.

He started small, sharing his tales in hushed whispers within Shaya's small circle. As his confidence grew, so did his audience. He began telling his stories in the shadowed corners of the city, his words echoing through the hidden tunnels, weaving their way into the hearts of the desperate and the weary. He spoke of Aldar's cruelty, but he also highlighted the absurdity of his reign, his overconfidence, and the inherent flaws in his strategies. He weaved subtle hints of discontent within Aldar's ranks, whispers of betrayal and looming doom, seeding doubts and fears amongst the enemy soldiers.

His words weren't solely focused on the enemy. He also celebrated the strengths of the Coronians, highlighting their resourcefulness, their courage, and their unwavering spirit. He created epic poems celebrating the achievements of the resistance, even the smallest victories, transforming mundane acts of sabotage into legendary feats of daring. He recounted tales of those who had fallen, transforming their sacrifice into a beacon of inspiration, fueling the resolve of the living.

His impact was undeniable. The city, initially paralyzed by fear, began to stir. The Coronians, inspired by Gerald's narratives, found renewed strength and purpose. His words were weapons, as potent as any sword or bow, carving a path through the despair that had threatened to engulf them.

Beyond storytelling, Gerald demonstrated a quiet leadership, based on empathy and understanding. He worked alongside the other members of the resistance, sharing their burdens and celebrating their successes. He learned from Shaya's strategic brilliance, from Finn's meticulous planning, from Falon's herbal expertise, and from Elara's subtle magical interventions. He discovered a hidden strength within himself.

He participated in clandestine operations, his knowledge of the human psyche proving as valuable as his storytelling skills. He learned to move silently through the shadowed alleys, to decipher coded messages, and to blend seamlessly into the city's underbelly. His presence in the field provided not only courage but also a level of insight into Aldar's strategy, his understanding of human behavior providing a unique edge.

One of the more daring operations saw Gerald leading a small team into the heart of Aldar's camp. Their mission: to disrupt the enemy's communication lines. Armed with Falon's sleep draught and disguised in scavenged enemy uniforms, they slipped through the enemy lines like phantoms. Gerald, relying on his understanding of human psychology, strategically positioned himself near the main communication tent, subtly influencing conversations with carefully placed remarks, sowing seeds of doubt and confusion. While his companions disrupted the communication lines, Gerald cleverly amplified the already present dissent within the camp, planting the seeds of rebellion with his words.

Another mission involved the liberation of more captive Coronian prisoners held in the dungeons beneath Aldar's fortress. It was a perilous undertaking, but Gerald's calm demeanor and strategic thinking proved invaluable. He devised a plan that combined Falon's potent sleeping draughts, Finn's tactics, and Elara's subtle magical illusions to create a diversion, allowing them to free dozens of prisoners.

The siege continued, the battles raging both above and below ground. But as the days turned into weeks, the balance of power began to shift. The underground resistance, once a small, flickering flame, had grown into a raging fire, fueled by Gerald's leadership, Shaya's strategy, and the staunch spirit of the Coronians themselves. The city, once on the brink of collapse, was now standing defiant, its hope rekindled, its resilience tested and proven. The siege of Coron was far from over, but Gerald, the writer from another world, had become an integral part of its improbable salvation. His journey was far from complete, yet his impact on the fight for Coron was undeniable. The writer was now, a warrior, a beacon of hope in the heart of a besieged city.

The ever-dwindling supplies were a constant gnawing worry. Shaya, her face worn with grim determination, presented the bleak reality during a clandestine meeting held deep within the labyrinthine tunnels beneath the city. The stores of food and medicinal herbs were critically low. The relentless siege had cut off their supply lines, and the meager resources remaining were barely enough to sustain the city for another week. The faces around the table, illuminated by the flickering lantern light, reflected the gravity of the situation – Falon's usually cheerful countenance was clouded with worry, Finn's hint of desperation, and even Elara's calm demeanor was frayed.

"We cannot simply wait for reinforcements," Shaya stated, her voice firm despite the tremor in her hands. "Aldar will not grant us that luxury. We must act, and we must do it now."

Gerald, spoke up. "What options do we have, Shaya? Our defenses are stretched thin, and Aldar's army is relentless."

"Desperate situation call for desperate solutions," Finn replied, his voice low and measured. "We must disrupt more of Aldar's supply lines. We must strike at the heart of his operations, weaken his forces, and buy ourselves time."

The discussion that followed was a tense ballet of strategic planning and determination. The options presented were all fraught with peril, each gamble with potentially devastating consequences. One suggestion involved another daring night raid on Aldar's main supply depot; a heavily fortified structure located deep within enemy territory. Another focused on sabotaging Aldar's siege weaponry, a mission that required infiltrating the enemy camp undetected. Yet another proposed a desperate attempt to reestablish contact with neighboring kingdoms, a perilous journey through Aldar's controlled territories.

The risks were immense. Failure could mean the complete collapse of the city's defenses and the utter annihilation of the resistance. But inaction was a form of slow suicide, a gradual descent into starvation and surrender.

The night of the operation was shrouded in a thick, oppressive fog, providing an ideal cover for their clandestine activities. The air filled with anticipation of imminent action, the silence broken only by the distant rumble of Aldar's war machines and the hushed whispers of the conspirators.

Finn's team moved like shadows, navigating the intricate labyrinth of tunnels that crisscrossed beneath the city. Their mission was precise and perilous: to disable the catapults without triggering an alarm. Falon's sleep draught played a crucial role, allowing them to neutralize the guards without bloodshed. Elara's magic wove a veil of illusion, masking their movements and diverting the attention of patrols. The operation was a success, several catapults were rendered useless, significantly weakening Aldar's siege capabilities.

Meanwhile, Gerald's operation was more subtle but no less crucial. He had infiltrated the enemy camp disguised as a scout, he spent hours observing the enemy soldiers, carefully studying their dynamics, their fears, and their vulnerabilities. He quietly manipulated conversations, planting seeds of doubt and discontent, and subtly amplifying existing tensions. He whispered tales of Aldar's downfall, exaggerating the stories of deserters and betrayals. He planted rumors of imminent defeat.

The results of his subtle manipulations were almost immediate. Rumors started spreading like wildfire through the enemy camp, fueled by Gerald's insidious narratives. Soldiers started questioning Aldar's leadership, and their confidence waned. The once disciplined army showed signs of cracking, its effectiveness significantly diminished.

Gerald's deception was a high stakes gamble. One wrong move could expose his identity and lead to his capture or worse. His every move was a calculated risk; a tightrope walk between success and failure. He skillfully played on the existing insecurities and fears within the camp, turning their own anxieties against them.

The combined effects of Finn's sabotage and Gerald's psychological manipulation created a significant shift in the balance of power. Aldar's siege, once relentless and unstoppable, began to falter. His army, plagued by internal strife and weakened by the loss of its most effective siege weapons, lost its relentless momentum.

As dawn broke, a sense of cautious optimism spread through the underground resistance. Their desperate measures had paid off. They had bought themselves precious time.

The siege wasn't over, but the tide had begun to turn. The Coronians, inspired by their recent success, found renewed hope and determination. Gerald, the writer from another world, had once again proven his worth, not just as a storyteller, but as a strategist and a growing warrior, his unconventional skills proving more effective than any conventional weapon. The siege continued, but Coron, once teetering on the brink of destruction, now stood a little taller, its resilience fortified by desperate measures and unexpected heroism. The writer who fell into another world was quickly becoming the unexpected hero this world needed.

8

Aldar's True Power

The respite afforded by the successful night raid was short lived. The air crackled with a renewed sense of urgency as Lyra convened another clandestine meeting. The success had been tactical, a temporary reprieve, but Aldar's forces remained a formidable threat. The conversation centered on Morack, Aldar's enigmatic sorcerer, whose dark magic fueled much of the siege's relentless brutality. Lyra, her gaze intense, laid out their next objective: uncovering Morack's weaknesses.

"We know little of Morack," Lyra began, her voice low and serious. "His power is evident, but its source, its limits... these are unknown. Our informants suggest he operates from a hidden fortress nestled within the Black Forest, a place shrouded in an unnatural mist." Finn chimed in. "Ancient texts mention a sorcerer by that name, associated with forbidden rituals and dark pacts. But these accounts are fragmented, offering little in terms of concrete vulnerabilities."

Falon, her brow furrowed in concentration, added, "My grandmother spoke of Morack. She claimed his magic was tied to a specific artifact, a relic of immense power, corrupted by dark forces. She called it the Obsidian Heart."

Gerald, his mind racing, found himself drawn to the cryptic details. The Obsidian Heart... the name resonated with a strange familiarity, a faint echo from a forgotten dream or a half-remembered story. He couldn't quite place it, but the feeling of unease lingered.

"We need to gather more information," Elara said, her voice calm but resolute. "We need to learn more about this Obsidian Heart, its properties, and its connection to Morack's magic. Only then can we hope to understand his weaknesses."

The ensuing discussion detailed a plan for infiltration. Knowing the Black Forest was a treacherous place, riddled with magical traps and guarded by creatures born of shadow and nightmares. Stealth and cunning were paramount. Finn, with his knowledge of ancient lore and hidden pathways, would lead the scouting expedition. Falon's herbal remedies would provide protection against the forest's more insidious dangers. Elara's magic would act as a shield and a guide, masking their presence and navigating the treacherous terrain. Gerald, with his newfound abilities, would be vital during their journey through the forest.

The Black Forest was a place of ancient gloom, filled with the festering odor of decay and an air of menace. Trees creaked eerily in the wind, and a thick creeping fog blurred vision and muffled sounds, intensifying the sense of unease.

They moved silently and cautiously through the forest. Finn, drawing on past experience, led them safely past traps and watched for hidden dangers. Elara stayed alert, preparing antidotes and protective spells to guard them from the forest's perils.

Gerald, observing everything with a keen eye, noticed details that others might have missed. The subtle shifts in the atmosphere, the barely perceptible changes in the vegetation, the almost imperceptible movements in the shadows— all clues that spoke of Morack's presence, a subtle but pervasive energy emanating from the heart of the forest.

They overcame many obstacles, both physical and magical, contending with eerie creatures and shadowy forces that tested their resolve. Navigating treacherous terrain and braving supernatural storms, they pressed on, driven by their mission for the fate of Coron. After a long and perilous journey, they reached Morack's fortress towering monolith structure surrounded by a shimmering magical barrier that manifested the sorcerer's formidable Power, emitting a disquieting or unnerving energy. They would have to approach with extreme caution.

Their infiltration required a careful and calculated approach. Finn, using his knowledge of arcane runes, discovered a hidden weakness in the magical barrier, a subtle flaw in its construction. He carefully manipulated the runes, disrupting the barrier's energy flow and creating a temporary opening. They slipped through the opening, entering the fortress with the silent efficiency of seasoned spies.

The fortress was a labyrinth of twisting corridors and chambers, filled with cryptic symbols and particular artifacts. The air hung heavy with the scent of incense and the chilling presence of dark magic. They moved cautiously, their senses on high alert, navigating the treacherous hallways.

Their investigation revealed that Morack's power was not solely based on his own abilities but was closely linked to a number of ancient artifacts. At the center of the chamber stood a an illustrious obsidian crystal, emanating a rhythmic energy, its surface inscribed with ancient runes that periodically shifted in appearance giving an unsettling effect on those present.

As they observed the Morack, they also discovered a chilling truth about his history. He had not always been a sorcerer of darkness. Inscriptions on the walls revealed his past: a once respected scholar who had sought to unlock the secrets of the universe, a quest that had ultimately corrupted him and twisted his soul. His obsession with the Obsidian crystal had irrevocably altered his fate, transforming him into the malevolent sorcerer he had become. Further investigation showed that the Obsidian crystal was both Morack's power source and prison. Its dark magic kept him aligned with evil and fueled his abilities by drawing energy from the environment but also made him dependent on it. Destroying the crystal could be essential to stopping Morack yet doing so risked releasing catastrophic dark energy.

Learning Morack's weakness and his dark past gave them an edge against Aldar but also left them with a serious dilemma. As they returned to the Sanctuary through the deepening shadows of the Black Forest, they faced a dangerous path requiring careful planning and tough decisions.

While gathering in the Sanctuary's chamber the flickering candlelight cast long, dancing shadows across the ancient parchments spread across the Sanctuary's worn wooden table. Finn, his brow furrowed in concentration, traced a finger along faded glyphs, his lips moving silently as he deciphered the archaic script. The air hummed with a quiet intensity, an evident sense of anticipation hanging heavy in the room. Elara, her eyes closed, seemed to be drawing strength from some unseen source, a subtle energy emanating from her fingertips. Falon, meticulously cleaned and cataloged the recovered scrolls, her nimble fingers moving with practiced ease. Gerald, meanwhile, found himself captivated by the sheer volume of information – a chaotic tapestry woven from fragmented histories, cryptic prophecies, and tantalizing clues. These texts were ancient relics from lost civilizations, containing accounts of powerful magic and mythical beings. Some detailed Aldar's rise, his quest for domination, and the realms he conquered. Others outlined his dark rituals, shadowy alliances, and weaknesses that could be exploited. One scroll described Aldar's origins.

A text outlined a ritual performed under a blood moon that boosted Aldar's powers. Using his knowledge of ancient languages and magic, Finn decoded the steps, ingredients, and timing described in cryptic detail. He discovered that Aldar's strength came from these celestial rituals rather than innate ability, making understanding and disrupting the process crucial for weakening Aldar.

Yet another parchment spoke of a legendary artifact – not the Obsidian crystal associated with Morack, but a relic of immense power linked directly to Aldar himself: the Serpent's Eye. This mystical gemstone, the text described, was the source of Aldar's inherent magical strength. It was said to have been forged in the heart of a dying star, imbued with the raw power of creation itself. The gemstone possessed a peculiar vulnerability: its power was inextricably linked to Aldar's own life force. If the Serpent's Eye were somehow damaged or destroyed, Aldar's magical capabilities would be drastically diminished, leaving him vulnerable to attack. The location of the Serpent's Eye was a closely guarded secret, lost to time and shrouded in mystery. The text offered only cryptic clues, allusions to ancient ruins and forgotten landscapes.

Hours melted into a blur of frantic research, their combined knowledge forming a mosaic of Aldar's past, his strengths, and critically, his weaknesses. They uncovered details of his personality, identifying patterns in his actions, his motives, and his methods. They learned that while Aldar was ruthless and ambitious, this knowledge, they realized, could be used to their advantage.

As dawn broke over the Sanctuary, they compiled their findings. The ancient texts provided valuable insights into Aldar's vulnerabilities and motivations. This knowledge presented opportunities for strategic manipulation, enabling them to exploit his weaknesses and disrupt his ranks.

The discovery of the Serpent's Eye's was particularly significant. It offered a tangible target, a specific weakness to exploit. Locating the gemstone would be a daunting task, requiring a perilous journey into uncharted territory. They needed a plan, a well-calculated strategy that would allow them to locate and neutralize the Serpent's Eye, weakening Aldar along with Morack's power and potentially paving the way for a decisive victory.

Falon reminded them of the immediate threat posed by Morack and his Obsidian crystale. While Aldar's ultimate defeat might hinge on finding the Serpent's Eye, neutralizing Morack remained a pressing concern. His dark magic continued to bolster Aldar's forces, sustaining the siege and preventing any meaningful progress.

Elara, her eyes gleaming with determination, proposed a two-pronged approach. One team, led by Finn, would focus on locating the Serpent's Eye, navigating treacherous landscapes and uncovering ancient secrets. Another, consisting of Falon and Gerald, would finalize their plan to exploit Morack's vulnerability, aiming to neutralize the Obsidian Heart and cripple Aldar's primary magical support. She herself, with her vast magical abilities, would act as a conduit of communication and support, coordinating their actions and lending assistance as needed. Gerald, adapting to his new reality, found purpose as a vital member of the resistance. His skills became key in their struggle against Aldar's power. The ancient texts gave them hope and a plan, preparing them for the difficult battle for Coron. As dawn arrived, they continued to look over a unique parchment describing Aldar's ritual featured swirling glyphs radiating faint energy. Finn quietly translated its arcane text, revealing the ritual as a recurring process performed under a blood moon. Though exhausting and painful, it granted Aldar a substantial boost in power and control over his realms.

The ritual's components were as chilling as its process. The parchment detailed a complex concoction of rare herbs, each harvested under specific astrological conditions, their potent essences blended to create a volatile elixir. The text further described the need for specific sacrificial offerings, creatures imbued with potent magical energies, their life force channeled into fueling Aldar's dark power. The ritual's location was equally significant – a desolate plateau known as the Widow's Peak, a place shrouded in perpetual twilight, where the veil between worlds thinned, allowing for a more potent connection to the dark energies that Aldar commanded. The timing was paramount, the precise alignment of stars and planets needed to create a celestial gateway, funneling primal forces into Aldar's very being.

"The ritual," Finn explained, his voice low and grave, "is not merely a source of amplified power; it's the very foundation of Aldar's dominion. Without it, his control weakens, his magical abilities diminish. It's a constant, cyclical drain on the world's energies, yet it's also the key to his survival."

Elara, her eyes fixed on the parchment, added, "The text suggests that the ritual's demands increase with each cycle. The sacrifices become more potent, the required energies more intense. Aldar is trapped in a vicious cycle, constantly needing to replenish his power, perpetually drawing from the life force of Coron and its inhabitants."

Falon, chimed in, "So, disrupting the ritual becomes our priority. If we can prevent him from completing the next cycle, we cripple his power significantly. But how do we accomplish that? The Widow's Peak is heavily guarded; it's an almost impenetrable fortress."

The ensuing discussion was intense and focused. They dissected every detail of the ritual, searching for a point of vulnerability to exploit. They debated various strategies, weighing the risks and rewards of each approach. Gerald, surprisingly, found his analytical skills invaluable, his experience with intricate plots and character motivations translating surprisingly well into formulating a strategic plan to counter Aldar's ritual.

The most significant detail, they concluded, was the timing. The ritual could only be performed under the blood moon, and the specific alignment of planets required made the window of opportunity narrow. It was a tight timeframe that demanded precision, careful planning, and flawless execution. Furthermore, the ritual was tied to specific geographical locations and the precise arrangement of the sacrificial elements around the altar. Interfering with these elements could disrupt the flow of magical energy, preventing the ritual's completion.

"We need to infiltrate Widow's Peak," Elara stated decisively, her voice firm and resolute. "We need to disrupt the ritual before it begins."

"But how?" Falon questioned, her brow furrowed in concern. "It's virtually impossible to sneak past Aldar's forces undetected."

Finn suggested a diversionary tactic. He proposed sending a small detachment to create a distraction, luring Aldar's forces away from Widow's Peak while the main group stealthily infiltrated the location and interfered with the preparations for the dark ritual. The distraction would have to be significant enough to draw a substantial portion of Aldar's forces away from the crucial ritual.

"A daring strategy," Gerald observed, "but potentially effective. We need to create a diversion that's both credible and irresistible to Aldar."

The subsequent hours were spent refining their plan. They meticulously studied maps, charting routes and identifying potential obstacles. They analyzed Aldar's known tactics and strategies, anticipating his responses and developing countermeasures. Gerald, drawing on his experience as a writer, crafted a series of misleading signals, creating a deceptive narrative that would lure Aldar into a false sense of security and redirect his forces.

The strategy was to fabricate a fake threat, distracting Aldar from Widow's Peak by simulating a large attack on a key supply or communications site. Using deceptive magic, they would create a convincing illusion of a major military assault. The plan was risky, but they had little alternative. The ritual was a matter of urgency; delay meant a strengthening of Aldar's power, making future conflict even more perilous. The success of their mission hinged on the element of surprise, the ability to deceive Aldar completely, and the precise coordination of their actions.

With the plan in place, the team prepared for the inevitable confrontation. They gathered the necessary supplies, sharpened their weapons, and bolstered their defenses. Elara prepared a series of protective enchantments, enhancing their speed, their stealth, and their resilience. Finn focused his energy on developing the deceptive illusion, and counter strategies should they need a change in plans. Falon ensured that their equipment was in top condition, ready for the coming battle.

Gerald, surprisingly, his ability to construct compelling and believable stories proved unexpectedly relevant in their mission. He helped craft the illusionary elements to create a highly believable threat, using his imagination to construct detailed scenarios that would appear genuine to Aldar's forces.

The initial euphoria of formulating a plan to disrupt Aldar's ritual at Widow's Peak quickly faded as a chilling realization dawned upon them. Their strategy, while ambitious and potentially effective, hinged on a crucial assumption – that disrupting the ritual was enough to significantly weaken Aldar. But what if Aldar's power stemmed from a source beyond the ritual itself? What if the ritual was merely a conduit, a means to amplify a far more potent, underlying force?

This question, posed by Elara during a tense moment of quiet contemplation, sent a ripple of unease through the group. They had focused solely on the ritual, believing it to be the cornerstone of Aldar's power. But Elara had un-earthed a cryptic passage in ancient texts, a hidden detail that had eluded them until now. This passage hinted at a mystical artifact, an object of immense power, hidden deep within the heart of Coron itself.

The passage spoke of "The Heart of Coron," a legendary artifact said to possess unimaginable magical energies. It was rumored to be the source of Coron's own inherent magic, a conduit channeling the raw energies of the realm. According to legend, whoever controlled the Heart of Coron controlled the very essence of the kingdom, wielding its power for their own ends. The passage implied that the Serpents Eye could tap into the Heart of Coron, using it as the ultimate source of his immense power, with the blood moon ritual serving only to amplify this already formidable source.

"If this is true," Finn stated, his voice barely a whisper, "then our plan is doomed to failure. Disrupting the ritual will only temporarily weaken him; he'll simply draw more power from the Heart of Coron to replenish his reserves."

Falon, immediately voiced her concern, "But how do we even find this 'Heart of Coron'? The passage offers no clues as to its location. It's like searching for a needle in a cosmic haystack."

The revelation weighed heavily on them, rendering their careful planning suddenly inadequate. Their initial opti-mism gave way to dread as they realized Aldar's power came not just from dark magic, but from a deeper, ancient source within Coron. Still, Gerald found hope; relying on his analytical mind, he suggested searching the ancient texts for clues about the Heart of Coron, suspecting overlooked hints remained.

The group spent the remaining hours before their planned infiltration of Widow's Peak poring over the ancient texts. They meticulously searched for every hidden reference, every cryptic allusion, every fragment of information that could lead them to the Heart of Coron. Finn, with his expertise in ancient languages and arcane lore, painstakingly translated the most obscure passages, while Elara and Falon aided in the search, their knowledge of Coronian history and geography proved invaluable. Gerald, armed with his keen eye for detail and his ability to discern patterns, helped piece together fragments of information, connecting seemingly unrelated details to form a coherent picture.

As the blood moon cast its ominous glow over the landscape, they finally found a significant breakthrough. A hidden passage, barely visible beneath a layer of dust and decay, described the Heart of Coron not as a physical object but as a metaphysical entity, an energy source resonating within a specific location – the Royal Crypts beneath the ruins of Old Coron.

The Royal Crypts, long abandoned and rumored to be haunted, were considered a sacred site, off limits to all but the highest nobility. Their location, hidden deep within a network of forgotten tunnels and subterranean passages, made them exceptionally difficult to access. Moreover, they were believed to be protected by ancient wards and magical barriers, designed to safeguard the sacred site from intruders.

"This complicates things significantly," Finn stated, his voice laced with apprehension. "The Royal Crypts are virtually impenetrable. We face an even greater challenge than we initially anticipated."

Elara remained resolute. "We have no choice. If Aldar's power is truly rooted in the Heart of Coron, then we must find a way to reach the Royal Crypts and sever its connection to it. It's our only hope of defeating him permanently."

Falon added, "But getting past the wards and the protective barriers will require significant magical power and a profound understanding of ancient Coronian magic. I hope we are adequately prepared."

The ensuing discussion was tense and sobering. They assessed their capabilities and limitations, realizing that their initial plan, focused solely on disrupting the ritual, was now secondary to the far greater challenge of infiltrating the Royal Crypts and confronting the source of Aldar's power. Gerald suggested a new multipronged plan: one team would of highly skilled Coronian fighters would cause a distraction at Widow's Peak, while an elite group, Elara, Finn, and himself would stealthily infiltrate the Royal Crypts, using magic to bypass wards. The decision was not easy. It meant splitting their forces, increasing their vulnerability and the risk of failure. But the stakes were too high to ignore.

As the blood moon reached its zenith, casting an eerie crimson glow across the landscape, the team prepared for their dual missions. They were embarking on a mission of monumental significance, a mission that would determine the balance of power in the realms. The true source of Aldar's power had been revealed, and the path to victory now lay through the heart of Old Coron, through the perilous and guarded depths of the Royal Crypts.

The plan, once laid bare, felt less like a strategic maneuver and more like a desperate gamble. The initial euphoria of a seemingly foolproof strategy had vanished, replaced by a sobering awareness of its inherent risks. Their mission was twofold: a diversionary attack at Widow's Peak to draw Aldar's attention, and a simultaneous infiltration of the Royal Crypts to sever his connection to the Heart of Coron. Success hinged on perfect timing and flawless execution, a precarious balance that left little room for error.

Elara, her face etched with grim determination, outlined the specifics. "The diversionary attack will be led by Falon," she explained, her voice sharp and precise. "She will assemble a team of skilled warriors from within the Sanctuary, utilizing guerilla tactics to harass Aldar's forces at Widow's Peak. The objective isn't to win a decisive battle, but to create enough chaos and confusion to divert his attention away from the Royal Crypts."

Falon, spoke and nodded. "I can choose a team of warriors known for their speed, agility, and experience in unconventional warfare. We will use smoke bombs, misdirection, and quick strikes to maximize our impact and minimize casualties. It will be messy, dangerous, but necessary and we will keep the enemy engaged."

The plan to infiltrate the Royal Crypts required a different approach entirely. It demanded stealth, precision, and a deep understanding of ancient Coronian magic. Gerald, Finn, and Elara would constitute the infiltration team, guided by Finn's expert knowledge of the underground tunnels leading to the Crypts. They would need to navigate a labyrinthine network of forgotten passages, evade lethal traps, and overcome powerful wards guarding the sacred site.

"The wards are ancient and formidable," Finn cautioned, stroking his beard thoughtfully. "They respond to specific magical signatures, and any attempt to force them will trigger potent countermeasures. We'll need to approach this delicately, using subtle magic and cunning to bypass them."

Gerald, despite his lack of formal magical training, was confident in his ability to contribute. His writer's mind, accustomed to dissecting intricate narratives and predicting plot twists, would be invaluable in deciphering the ambiguous clues that would help them navigate the Crypts. His analytical skills could be as potent as any spell in this situation.

The following days were consumed by relentless preparation. Falon's team underwent rigorous training, perfecting their guerilla tactics and honing their skills in close quarters combat. Meanwhile, Gerald, Finn, and Elara immersed themselves in the ancient texts, poring over every cryptic passage, every cryptic symbol, every hidden detail that could offer insights into the Crypts' defenses.

Elara's knowledge of ancient Coronian helped to decipher intricate runes and arcane symbols, revealing sequences of spells and rituals that seemed to hold the key to disabling the wards.

Finn, meanwhile, focused on the layout of the Crypts. The ancient maps, fragmented and incomplete, were painstakingly pieced together, revealing a complex network of tunnels, chambers, and hidden passages. He identified potential chokepoints, escape routes, and hidden pathways, information that would prove critical during their infiltration.

The night of the blood moon arrived, an ominous crimson glow painting the sky. Tension grew as the two teams prepared for their respective missions. Falon's team, clad in dark armor and armed with their unconventional weapons, moved silently from the Sanctuary through the shadows, their footsteps muffled by the soft earth of the forest floor. They positioned themselves for the assault at Widow's Peak.

Gerald, Finn, and Elara, made their way to Old Coron armed with their knowledge and their spells. They descended into the labyrinthine tunnels leading to the Royal Crypts. The air grew cold and damp as they ventured deeper into the earth, the silence broken only by the drip, drip, drip of water echoing through the vast chambers.

The first challenge came in the form of a complex magical barrier, a shimmering wall of energy pulsating with ancient power. Elara, drawing upon her vast knowledge of Coronian magic, began to chant an ancient incantation, her voice resonating with the power of forgotten ages. The runes, carefully selected from the ancient texts, were traced in the air, the shimmering barrier flickering in response.

The incantation was a delicate dance, a balance of rhythm and precision. A single mistake would trigger a powerful backlash, but Elara's years of experience and expertise allowed her to maintain the intricate rhythm, the barrier finally dissolving before them, leaving a momentary breach.

They moved swiftly, navigating the tunnels with practiced ease. Finn's knowledge of the underground passages was proving to be priceless, as they avoided hidden traps and treacherous pitfalls. They encountered other wards and barriers, but through a combination of cunning and careful magical maneuvers, they managed to overcome them, each success fueling their determination to press on.

Their progress was slow but steady, each step forward bringing them closer to their goal. But the deeper they ventured, the more ominous the atmosphere became. A sense of ancient dread seemed to cling to the very stones, the shadows alive with whispers and unseen presences. They were venturing into the heart of Coron's darkest secrets, a place where the boundary between the living and the dead blurred.

As they finally approached the main chamber of the Royal Crypts, a chilling realization dawned upon them. The final barrier was not a magical ward, but a physical obstacle a colossal stone door loomed before them, a final, insurmountable obstacle in their path. Its surface, etched with intricate runes that pulsed with faint, shimmering light, seemed to hum with ancient power. The air crackled with an unnerving energy, a tangible manifestation of the magic that bound the door shut. Their progress had brought them to a point of no return, a final test of their skills and determination before they could locate the Heart of Coron and confront Aldar's power at its source. Their hearts beating with anticipation, the culmination of their risky plan yet to come.

Gerald ran a hand along the cold, rough stone, tracing the swirling patterns of the runes with his fingertips. He felt a faint thrumming vibration, a silent song of power that resonated deep within his bones.

"This is more than just a lock," Finn muttered, his voice barely a whisper in the echoing chamber. "This is a ward, woven into the very structure of the stone. It's designed to repel intruders, to keep unwanted guests from entering the heart of the Royal Crypts."

Elara, her eyes narrowed in concentration, examined the runes more closely. "The runes are a combination of protective and defensive spells," she observed. "They are layered, intricately interwoven, making them incredibly difficult to bypass. A brute force approach would be suicidal."

Gerald stepped forward. "We need a different strategy. We can't force our way through; we have to find a way to unlock it." He studied the runes again, searching for patterns, connections, anything that could provide a clue. He began searching for the underlying logic, the hidden key to unlock this magical puzzle.

After what felt like hours, but was in reality only minutes, Gerald's eyes lit up. "I think I see it," he exclaimed, pointing to a sequence of seemingly insignificant runes nestled amongst the more prominent ones. "These runes... they're a sequence, a code of sorts. They're not a defensive measure; they're a key."

Finn and Elara exchanged a look of skeptical curiosity. "A code?" Finn questioned. "How can, you be sure?"

"Look closely," Gerald urged, tracing the sequence with his finger. "The pattern... it's reminiscent of the ancient Coronian alphabet. But it's not a word, not a phrase. It's a sequence of numbers. A numerical key."

Elara, her magical senses heightened, confirmed his observation. "You're right. These runes represent a numerical sequence. But what does it unlock?"

The next few hours were a blur of frantic activity. Gerald, working tirelessly, translated the numerical sequence into a series of actions. He theorized that the runes represented a specific order of manipulating a series of hidden mechanisms within the stone door itself. Finn, with his vast knowledge of ancient Coronian mechanisms and engineering, helped decipher Gerald's instructions. Elara, with her delicate touch and magical sensitivity, carefully manipulated the hidden mechanisms, guided by Gerald's precise instructions.

The process was painstaking and fraught with danger. A single wrong move could trigger the powerful defensive wards surrounding the door, unleashing a devastating magical backlash. But with each correct step, a subtle click or shift in the stone indicated progress. They worked as a team, their combined skills and knowledge complementing each other perfectly.

Finally, after what seemed like an eternity, the last mechanism clicked into place. A low rumble echoed through the chamber as the colossal stone door began to slowly creak open. A wave of ancient energy washed over them, a palpable shift in the atmosphere. The door revealed a dark, imposing passage, leading deeper into the heart of the Royal Crypts.

Their infiltration mission was far from over. The passage opened into a dimly lit tunnel, winding deeper into the earth. The air was thick with the smell of damp earth and something else... something ancient and foreboding. The walls were lined with strange symbols and carvings, some depicting scenes of long forgotten battles and rituals, others etched with cryptic warnings and prophecies.

As they cautiously moved deeper into the tunnel, they encountered more challenges. Hidden traps, sprung by the slightest pressure or movement, threatened to send them plummeting into unseen chasms. Magical barriers shimmered and flickered, testing their skills and knowledge. They navigated the treacherous passage with the expertise only born from extensive preparation and painstaking study.

They were constantly having to adapt to their strategies. One section involved navigating a maze of moving walls that shifted unpredictably, requiring deft maneuvering and quick thinking to avoid being crushed or lost. In another area, they were confronted by a series of illusions, crafted to confuse and disorient their senses, testing the limits of their perception. They had to rely on their wits and instincts, as well as their combined knowledge and magical skills, to overcome the obstacles.

As they pressed on, a sense of uneasiness grew. The air grew colder, the silence more oppressive. They felt the weight of centuries of history and secrecy pressing down on them. The deeper they went, the more they felt like they were intruding on a sacred and forbidden space.

They eventually reached a vast cavern. In the center of the cavern, bathed in an eerie green glow, stood a towering obelisk made from obsidian. Intricate carvings covered its surface, depicting scenes of ancient kings and queens, battles, and ceremonies. At the base of the obelisk, a small pedestal with intricate shining stones surrounding a hollowed out area. As they neared the obelisk, an irractic energy radiated from it, making the air heavy. They realized they had entered the core of Old Coron.

The cavern's heavy silence was interrupted only by the steady sound of water dripping from hidden cracks. Casting an eeriness over the cavern, the magical power of Coron, a crystalline stone that once throbbed with ominous energy, was missing. Although they had cleverly managed to enter the Royal Crypts, they knew finding the crystalline stone was gravely important, and how Aldar intended to use the crystalline stone.

9

Infiltrating the Enemy

The next stage demanded a different kind of skill: deception in order to breach Aldar's main encampment.

"We can't simply walk into Aldar's camp," Elara stated, her voice low and serious. "His spies are everywhere. We need to blend in, to become invisible."

Finn nodded in agreement. "Disguise is essential. We need to look like we belong here, like we are part of Aldar's inner circle." "We need to study their attire, their mannerisms, their language. We need to become masters of impersonation." Gerald, with his experience crafting complex characters in his novels proved surprisingly relevant. He spent the next few days studying of Adlar's forces stationed along the edge of the Black Forest from a safe distance. They noted the subtle differences in clothing, the insignia that denoted loyalty and allegiance, and the specific styles of weaponry carried by each of the different warriors. He even studied the way they walked, talked, and interacted with each other. Every detail, no matter how insignificant it seemed, was meticulously recorded in Gerald's notebook.

For their disguises, they relied on Elara's magic and Finn's craftsmanship. Elara, with her mastery of illusion and transformation, subtly altered their appearances. She enchanted simple tunics and cloaks, shaping them to fit the soldiers' uniforms, while Finn, with his skill in forging and crafting, replicated the insignia and weaponry. Gerald, always the meticulous observer, noticed subtle differences in the soldiers' speech patterns. The soldiers from the northern regions spoke with a harsh, guttural accent, while those from the southern provinces had a softer, more melodious tone. He studied their vocabulary, their idioms, and their slang. He even mimicked their postures and gestures.

The preparation on their disguises were complete. Each disguise went beyond costumes, reflecting complete transformations that suited each role of the four brave fighters of Coron. They didn't just act—they fully embodied their characters, adopting convincing details and traits.

Their success in infiltration was due to a careful combination of disguise, deception, and teamwork. Their disguises made them invisible, their deception allowed them to maneuver through the enemy ranks, and their teamwork ensured they could support each other in every challenging situation. They faced countless close calls, narrow escapes, and moments of intense tension, all testing their abilities to the limit. The infiltration was successful, not because of brute force, but because of their skill in the art of disguise and deception. The stage was set for the final showdown.

They discovered Aldar's plans involved using a powerful artifact, the Serpents Eye, to amplify his dark magic, enabling him to conquer other realms and eventually Coron. Their goal was to locate this artifact and somehow disrupt Aldar's plans.

Aldar's camp outstretched before them, a sprawling labyrinth of tents, makeshift barracks, and hastily constructed fortifications, all illuminated by the flickering flames of countless fires. The sounds of boisterous brawls, moans, and the rhythmic clang of weapons being forged and sharpened painted a grim picture of their precarious situation. They were surrounded by hundreds, perhaps thousands, of the enemy, each a potential threat.

Their carefully crafted disguises, while effective, offered no absolute protection. A single slip, a misplaced word, a telltale movement—any of these could expose their deception and lead to swift, brutal capture. They moved with the calculated precision of a seasoned military unit, each step measured, each breath controlled. Falon, despite the added bulk of her disguise, moved with surprising agility, her diminutive size allowing her to slip through tight spaces and navigate the crowded pathways with ease. Her heightened senses, honed from years of living in the unforgiving terrain of the dwarven mountains, allowed her to have keen vision in the dim light.

Gerald, playing the role of a seasoned soldier, walked with a confident swagger, his eyes constantly scanning his surroundings, noting every detail, every potential hazard. He listened to the conversations around him, subtly adjusting his own speech to blend in, mirroring the accents and slang of the soldiers he encountered. His writer's mind, always active to anticipate questions and formulating appropriate responses. He found himself remarkably at ease in the role; his experience building believable characters in his fiction proved surprisingly useful in navigating this perilous reality.

At one point, Gerald found himself face to face with Morack, Aldar's sinister sorcerer. Morack, a tall, gaunt figure with piercing eyes and a sinister smile, regarded Gerald with suspicion. Gerald, playing the role of a loyal soldier, maintained his composure, offering a respectful salute and answering Morack's questions with carefully crafted responses.

Elara, in her healer's guise, moved with a quiet grace, her hands perpetually occupied, appearing to carefully check pouches of herbs and other medicinal supplies. She offered the occasional word of comfort to a wounded soldier, her voice soft and soothing, her touch gentle and reassuring. Her illusion magic, woven seamlessly into her disguise, subtly masked her natural elegance, giving her the worn appearance of a healer who had spent countless nights tending to the wounded. Her keen observation allowed her to spot potential danger and subtly guided their group away from trouble.

Finn, despite his altered appearance, cut an imposing figure, though his stooped posture and feigned limp masked his true strength. He moved with a deliberate slowness, his eyes perpetually watchful, his hand never far from the hilt of his concealed sword. His keen observation allowed him to anticipate potential threats and alert the group to impending danger, his craftsman's instincts helping him to identify the weak points in Aldar's defenses.

Their route was organized as a deliberate circuit, directing them toward Aldar's central tent, which functioned as the focal point of the opposing camp. The darkness provided concealment for their movements and intentions. They proceeded during the night, utilizing the shadows from tents and fortifications for cover while navigating around resting soldiers, moving forward with steady determination.

The camp teemed with activity even under the cloak of night. Sentries patrolled the perimeter, their torches casting long, dancing shadows that stretched and distorted the already confusing landscape. Groups of soldiers gathered around fires, their raucous laughter and drunken singing echoing through the camp, a stark contrast to the quiet determination of their mission. The aroma of roasting meat mingled with the stench of decay and unwashed bodies, creating a nauseating cocktail that assaulted their senses.

One particularly perilous encounter occurred as they navigated a narrow pathway between two tightly packed tents. A group of swaggering orgs emerged from one of the tents, their voices slurred, their movements unsteady. Their boisterous moans and crude grunts threatened to expose their presence, their stumbling gait potentially leading them directly into their path. Falon quickly diverted them into a nearby tent with a carefully placed distraction, a whispered rumor of a hidden cache of Aldar's ales. The soldiers, their attention captivated by the prospect of free drink, stumbled happily away, leaving the passage clear.

Another close call occurred near the central fire pit where a hideous Org sat surrounded by a group of other Orgs. The firelight revealed the intricacies of their disguises, putting them under immense scrutiny. Gerald, ever the master of improvisation, initiated a nonchalant conversation, casually casting unusual moans and groans that made no sense, but the Orgs just acknowledge him with a grunt, then turned their heads back toward the fire. The group, being surprised, waste no time by moving away from the hulking Orgs. Gerald and his companions persona's they were portraying had paid off.

As the night wore on, their movement through the encampment was a test of endurance, patience, and nerves. The fatigue gnawed at their bodies; the constant tension strained their minds. The fear of discovery loomed, a constant shadow lurking at the edges of their consciousness. Yet, they pressed on, driven by a shared purpose. Each successful maneuver, each close call averted, instilled a sense of growing confidence, a quiet triumph in the face of monumental odds.

They finally reached the perimeter of Aldar's central command, a large, fortified lodge that stood in stark contrast to the surrounding makeshift shelters. Guards stood sentinel at its entrance, their eyes constantly scanning the surroundings, their spears held at the ready. This was the culmination of their arduous mission, the final hurdle before they could infiltrate Aldar's inner circle and uncover the secrets of the Serpents Eye. The air buzzed with tension, the sounds punctuated only by the crackling of the campfires and the occasional rustle of leaves. Their hearts pounded in their chests, a rhythmic drumbeat that echoed their anticipation and fear. They had navigated the treacherous paths of Aldar's camp, avoiding capture, using the cover of darkness and disguise to mask their movements. But the true challenge lay ahead: penetrating the heart of the enemy's stronghold. The next phase of their mission demanded a different kind of skill, a different kind of courage.

The central structure, a behemoth of canvas and reinforced wood, pulsed with a low hum, a subtle vibration that resonated through the earth. From their concealed position, hidden behind a stack of discarded supplies, the group observed the comings and goings. Guards, heavily armed and alert, patrolled the perimeter with unwavering vigilance. Their immediate objective was not a direct confrontation, but infiltration. They needed information, specifics about Aldar's plans, the location of the Serpent's Eye – the mystical object that seemed to be the linchpin of his power and his conquest. This was a delicate dance, requiring stealth, and patience.

Elara, with her uncanny ability to blend into the background, discreetly approached a group of soldiers huddling around a fire. She feigned concern over their minor ailments, her voice soft and soothing, her touch gentle reassuring. While tending to their "ailments," she gleaned information about their recent activities and their movements. She learned of a recent supply run to a hidden cave system, a location strangely at odds with the typical supply routes. The implication was clear – something of strategic importance was being moved.

Meanwhile, Finn, with his imposing stature masked by his disguise, used his skills as a master craftsman to assess the tent's structure. He discovered a barely noticeable gap near the rear of the structure, a possible entry point for a stealthy infiltration. Once inside, Finn gathered what little information he found lying on a wooden table and hastily retreated from the tent. He regrouped with Gerald and Falon who were waiting for Elara.

Falon mentioned she noticed a specific sequence of hand signals exchanged between the guards, a silent communication method that likely conveyed important information or alerted to unusual activity. Her observations were particularly helpful in identifying potential blind spots in the guard's vigilance for their retreat.

Elara's newfound information regarding the supply runs to a cave system, created a clearer picture of Aldar's plans. It became apparent that the artifact wasn't simply being stored; it was being prepared for use. Finn remarked that the cave system location was noted in the papers he found within the main structure of the camp.

Over the course of several hours, they painstakingly gathered intelligence. The pieces of the puzzle slowly began to fall into place. Aldar's primary objective wasn't simply the conquest of Coron; he was preparing for a ritual, a dark and powerful magic ritual that was directly tied to the artifact. The cave system was not merely a storage location but a preparation chamber for this dark ritual, a place where the artifact was being empowered. The location itself was also a point of mystical significance, a nexus of dark energy which Aldar intended to harness for his nefarious purposes. This information revealed just how ambitious Aldar was. He planned to use the artifact not only to strengthen his hold over Coron, but also to access other realms and conquer them. The steady emanating coming from the main structure now made sense—it wasn't just powering the camp but was actually the sound of the artifact building up energy for an incredibly destructive spell. The team realized the urgency of their situation. They couldn't afford to linger. They had to act swiftly, before Aldar's plan reached fruition. The risk was immense, but the stakes were even higher.

This newly revealed location of the artifact's hiding place, entombed deep within the cave system, is only accessible through a series of treacherous tunnels and guarded by additional soldiers. The precise location of this chamber, however, was still shrouded in mystery. They needed to refine their intel, pinpointing the exact coordinates of the chamber. The team withdrew to their concealed observation post, fully aware of the significance of their findings. Equipped with critical intelligence, they could now formulate a structured plan. The subsequent phase of their mission would require discretion, strategic planning, and assertive action.

The first rays of dawn painted the sky in hues of bruised purple and hesitant gold, a stark contrast to the grim determination on the faces of the four infiltrators. As they slipped back into the shadows, a sudden shout ripped through the predawn stillness. A patrol, alerted by a misplaced footstep or a rustle of leaves – they couldn't be sure – had spotted a flicker of movement near the edge of their concealment.

Panic threatened to overwhelm them, but years of honed instincts took over. Falon, with a speed that belied her diminutive frame, scrambled behind a large pile of discarded weaponry, her small form swallowed by the shadows. Finn, his powerful frame, surprisingly agile, melted into the darkness behind a cluster of wagons, his disguise effectively concealing his movements. Elara, with a practiced grace, used a spell to alter the very texture of the air, creating a momentary shimmering distortion that masked her presence from the approaching guards.

Gerald was left exposed. He was the slowest, the least experienced in the arts of stealth. He had been so focused on scribbling notes about the overheard conversations a habit ingrained from his writer's instincts – that he hadn't accounted for the potential of detection. He lurked behind a low stack of wooden crates, the sound of his labored breathing a stark contrast to the tense silence around him. The guards, two heavily armed Orgs with fierce expressions, drew closer.

The guards were seemed suspicious. They exchanged sharp glances, their eyes scanning the area with an intensity that sent a chill down Gerald's spine. One of them moved towards the crates, his hand resting on the hilt of his sword, ready to investigate the potential hiding place. Gerald held his breath, his heart pounding a frantic rhythm in his chest, each second seemed to stretch into an eternity.

It was Elara who saved them. With a whispered word, a manipulation of the very fabric of reality, she conjured a shimmering mirage, a fleeting illusion of a small, harmless woodland creature flitting between the crates and the approaching guards. The Orgs eyes, momentarily captivated by the illusory spectacle, shifted their focus. Their suspicions, though not fully dispelled, were sufficiently diverted. The illusion vanished as quickly as it appeared, leaving no trace, but the Orgs were already moving on, their investigation seemingly concluded.

The close call served as a harsh reminder of their precarious position. They had come perilously close to exposure, a single misstep away from capture or worse. The initial elation at their intelligence gathering was replaced by a sober realization of the risks involved.

They needed formulate a plan. They needed to advance quickly into a perilous plan that would push the boundaries of their capabilities. After a long discussion, huddled in the relative safety of the forest's deeper recesses, decided on a bolder approach – a direct infiltration of the hidden cave system. The risk was significant, but the rewards outweighed the danger. The cave system offered a potential shortcut, a means of intercepting the artifact before Aldar could fully harness its power.

Their plan hinged on the disruption of Aldar's ritual preparations. They would use a combination of stealth, distraction, and their individual skills to navigate the treacherous tunnels and outwit the guards stationed within the cave system. Finn would use his knowledge of engineering to disable the cave's defenses, creating diversionary points to draw attention away from the others. Falon would scout the pathways ahead, identifying traps and patrol routes. Elara would use her magic to create diversions, misdirecting guards and masking their movements. And Gerald? Gerald would use his writer's mind to document everything, chronicling the events for posterity and providing real time updates to the team.

The excursion through the cave system was fraught with peril. They encountered narrow passageways, treacherous ravines, and seemingly endless tunnels that twisted and turned in a labyrinthine fashion. The dank air smelled of wet earth and a faint, sinister magic that lingered on the cave walls. The silence was broken only by the drip, drip, drip of water echoing through the cavernous spaces.

They navigated several near misses with patrols, employing a combination of stealth and diversion tactics. Elara used illusions, conjuring images of collapsing tunnels and terrifying beasts to distract the guards. Finn's stealth tactics aided them in bypassing several security checkpoints without detection. Falon's sharp hearing pinpointed the positions of hidden guards and predicted patrol patterns, preventing them from walking into ambushes further long their way.

They finally reached the artifact chamber; a vast cavern bathed in an unnatural light emanating from the mystical object itself. The one artifact, a crystalline sphere pulsing with dark energy, hovered in the center of the chamber, surrounded by elaborate ritualistic paraphernalia. Aldar's sorcerer, Morack, stood over the sphere, chanting in a guttural tongue, his face contorted in a grotesque mask of concentration. The air snapped with anticipation. This was it. The moment of truth. The culmination of their perilous trek, their narrow escapes, their daring infiltration. They were face to face with the source of Aldar's power, a single moment away from either triumph or utter destruction. The fate of Coron hung in the balance. They were finally within striking distance of victory. The next step would require more than courage and cunning – it would require a desperate gamble, a bold stroke that could either save Coron or cost them everything.

10

Confronting Morack

The cavern's air buzzed with energy. Morack, cloaked in shadow and arcane power, faced away from them, silhouetted by a glowing crystalline sphere. The sphere's hum sent a chill through Gerald, radiating dark magic.

Falon, being vigilant, held her breath, her hand resting lightly on the axe strapped to his back. Her usual boisterous spirit was subdued, replaced by a quiet intensity. Finn assessed the chamber, her eyes scanning for escape routes and potential vulnerabilities in Morack's defenses. Elara, her face pale but resolute, prepared herself, her hands glowing faintly with a protective light.

Gerald, meanwhile, felt a surge of adrenaline, a cocktail of fear and exhilaration coursing through his veins. He instinctively reached for his note pad, his fingers fumbling for the worn leather cover, a desperate need to record this pivotal moment overwhelming him. This wasn't just another scene; this was a climax, a confrontation that would determine the fate of an entire kingdom. And he, Gerald Weaver, the reluctant hero, was front and center.

Morack finally turned, his face a grotesque mask of ghastly features, his eyes burning with a sinister gleam. His robes, dark and flowing, seemed to writhe with an independent life, their edges shimmering with supernatural energy. He spoke, his voice, a rasping whisper that echoed through the cavern, a language Gerald couldn't understand yet felt in his very soul.

The duel began not with a clash of steel, but with a war of wills, a silent contest of magical energies. Elara was the first to act, launching a barrage of defensive spells, weaving a shimmering shield of protective light around the group. Morack responded with a wave of dark energy, a torrent of force that crashed against Elara's defenses, sending ripples of power that rocked the very foundations of the cavern.

Finn, seeing an opening, launched a series of cunningly leveraged movements with his sword designed to disrupt Morack's concentration. Elara's magic was precise and targeted, aiming to break through Morack's defenses with a strategic barrage rather than brute force. Explosions of light and fiery charges of energy erupted throughout the chamber, illuminating the intricate carvings on the cavern walls and momentarily revealing hidden details.

Falon, recognizing the opportunity, moved with surprising swiftness and precision. She wasn't a sorcerer, not in the traditional sense, but her years of experience fighting in the black forest had honed her instincts, granting her an uncanny ability to anticipate her opponent's moves. She closed the distance, leaping across the chaotic cavern floor of magical energies, her axe raised, ready to strike.

Morack proved to be a formidable opponent. He deflected Falon's attack with a flick of his wrist, sending the dwarf sprawling. His counterattack was swift and brutal, a surge of dark energy that sent Falon tumbling backward, leaving her momentarily stunned. Gerald watched, his heart pounding in his chest, a mixture of fear and awe washing over him as he witnessed this clash of titans.

Elara, seeing Falon falter, immediately launched another wave of protective magic, shielding her from Morack's relentless assault. The protective spell shimmered, straining under the pressure of Morack's power, but holding firm. It was a desperate defense, a fragile barrier against a torrent of dark magic.

Gerald, meanwhile, continued to document the events, his pen furiously scribbling across the pages of his notebook. He sketched the swirling patterns of magic, noting the shifts in Morack's expressions, capturing the desperate struggle unfolding before him. His writer's eye for detail allowed him to observe nuances others might have missed – the faint tremor in Morack's hand, the shift in his breathing pattern, the telltale signs of his magical reserves depleting.

The battle raged on, a chaotic dance of light and shadow, of defensive spells and counterattacks. Each clash of magic rocked the cavern, sending tremors through the ground. Dust rained from the ceiling, and the very air seemed to crackle with raw magical energy. Gerald could feel the intensity of the struggle, the palpable weight of the forces at play.

As the duel progressed, a pattern began to emerge. Morack's power was immense, raw and untamed, but it was also erratic, unpredictable. His attacks were powerful, but lacked finesse, relying on brute force rather than precision. In contrast, Elara's magic, though less powerful, was far more refined, exhibiting a precision and control Morack lacked.

Gerald realized that the key to defeating Morack wasn't to match his power but to exploit his weaknesses. His unpredictable nature was both his strength and his downfall. He needed to find a way to disrupt Morack's focus, to break his rhythm, to force him to make a mistake. A sudden thought struck him. He had been focusing on documenting the battle, but his skills as a writer could be used in a far more active role.

He quickly scribbled a note in his notebook, outlining a new strategy. He would use his words, his writing, as a weapon. He would weave a story, a narrative so compelling, so emotionally resonant, that it would disrupt Morack's focus and create an opening for a decisive strike.

He began to read aloud, his voice trembling at first, then growing stronger, filled with a rising intensity He painted a vivid picture of the kingdom's idyllic past, a sharp contrast to the darkness Morack embodied. He spoke of hope, of courage, of the enduring power of the Kingdom. The words hung in the air, a counterpoint to the chaotic clash of magical energies. Morack, initially dismissive, began to falter.

His attacks became less precise, his movements hesitant, his concentration wavering.

Elara and Finn seized the opportunity. They launched a coordinated assault, magic and combat strength striking with precision, targeting Morack's weakened defenses. The combined force of attack overwhelmed Morack, breaking through his defenses and sending him reeling. He stumbled back, his eyes wide with disbelief, his dark magic flickering and fading.

Falon, seizing the moment, launched a final, desperate attack, her axe striking Morack with devastating force. The sorcerer, weakened and disoriented, fell to his knees, his power dissipating like smoke in the wind. The crystalline stone, the connection between it and Morack had been broken, pulsed once, twice, and then fell with a faint hum. The air in the cavern, once thick with energy, felt lighter, clearer, almost hopeful. The silence that followed was profound, broken only by Gerald's ragged breathing. The fate of Coron hung precariously in the balance, but for now, at least, they had survived. When they gathered their senses, they noticed that Morack had gone.

The aftermath of the initial clash left a lingering silence, heavy with the residue of raw magical energy. Dust mites danced in the faint light filtering through cracks in the cavern ceiling, illuminating the grim scene. Falon lay bruised but conscious, her axe discarded beside her. Elara's protective shield flickered, slowly dissipating, leaving her visibly drained. Finn, being resourceful, was already examining the crystalline stone, his brow furrowed in concentration noting that it appeared to be still giving off energy.

Gerald, the initial shock of his translocation had been overwhelming, a sensory deluge that nearly shattered his sanity. Yet, within that chaos, something had shifted, something had awakened. Now, in the harsh light of this subterranean battlefield, the true extent of his abilities began to reveal themselves.

He felt a surge of power, a tingling sensation spreading from his fingertips to the crown of his head. It wasn't a physical strength, not in the way Falon possessed it, but an energy, a vibrant force that mirrored the very magic crackling around him. He could feel the pulsing rhythm of the crystalline sphere, even after its power had been subdued. He could sense the subtle shifts in the magical energies emanating from Elara, a silent conversation between their souls and the magic that bound them. He could even sense the lingering echoes of Morack's dark magic, a shadowy remnant of its former power.

His notebook, once a simple tool of his trade, now felt like an extension of himself, a vessel through which his abilities flowed. He touched its worn leather cover, feeling a warmth spreading through his hand, a connection that went beyond the physical. The pages seemed to thrum with a faint energy, whispering secrets, urging him to write, to record, to create.

Morack, though defeated, still posed a threat. His defeat wasn't absolute; it was a temporary setback, a momentary silence of his dark power. He could regenerate, reconstitute his power, and return with a vengeance. Gerald knew this intuitively. He saw it not in a prophetic vision, but in the subtle lingering echoes of Morack's magical presence. He felt the slivers of remaining dark energy, whispering to him of Morack's strength even without the Heart of Coron.

The fight had shown him his potential, but also his limitations. He couldn't unleash spells of fire and shadow like Elara. He couldn't wield an axe with the precision of Falon. His strength lay elsewhere, in the power of his words. This newfound understanding invigorated him. His next task was to understand the full extent of his abilities. He needed to learn to channel this newfound power, to control the flow of energy, to harness his innate gifts. He began writing short sentences in his notebook, focusing his intention on their effects. He wrote about the fading light in the cavern, and the space seemed to grow brighter, the light illuminating the Damp dark walls with new clarity.

Each small act of writing was a step toward mastery, a journey into the depths of his own potential. He realized that his ability wasn't limited to creating simple effects; it extended to manipulating the very fabric of reality. He could weave illusions, create distractions, even influence the behavior of others through carefully crafted narratives. He could rewrite the very story of this confrontation, potentially influencing what Morack next move.

His next experiment was audacious, even reckless. He focused his attention on the lingering tendrils of Morack's dark magic, attempting to write them out of existence. His pen moved with speed and purpose, the words flowing from his hand like a river of light. As he wrote, the shadowy residue of Morack's magic dissipated from the cavern, fading into nothingness. The cavern felt lighter, cleaner, free from the oppressive weight of the sorcerer's presence. He felt an exhilarating sense of triumph.

He could shape the future, prevent disasters, even guide the destiny of Coron. A single misplaced word, a poorly chosen phrase, could have unintended consequences. He was wielding a potent force, a double-edged sword that could create and destroy with equal ease. He needed to understand its limits, to learn how to wield it responsibly, tempering its raw energy with careful intention and precise skill.

His journey into Coron had begun with a simple act of translocation, but it had transformed him into something far more. The confrontation with Morack had been a turning point; it was the moment he became the key to Coron's salvation. The battle was far from over, but now he had a new weapon, a new understanding of himself and the true extent of his abilities, and a renewed sense of purpose in this fantastical realm.

Falon, despite the throbbing pain in her side where Morack's shadow claw had grazed her, pushed herself to her feet. Her usually boisterous laughter was absent, replaced by a grim determination etched onto her weathered face. She gripped the shaft of her axe, its dwarven steel still humming faintly with residual magical energy, a testament to the ferocity of the recent battle. Dust coated her braided hair and clothes, clinging to the sweat that was beaded on her forehead. She looked around at the scene of the aftermath; the remnants of the conflict scattered around the cavern.

Elara, her face pale but her eyes bright with resilience, leaned against a stalagmite, her breath coming in ragged gasps. The magical shield she had conjured to protect them was gone, leaving her visibly exhausted. Yet, there was no hint of fear in her gaze, only a steely resolve. Finn was busy examining the crystalline sphere, muttering to himself as he carefully assessed the damage. His nimble fingers traced the intricate carvings; his brow furrowed in deep concentration. He grabbed the stone and placed it in his satchel.

Gerald watched as his companions showed remarkable courage and ingenuity, feeling a deep respect for them. Their unwavering determination in the midst of overwhelming challenges inspired him profoundly. He realized that his own strength was closely tied to their willpower, their resilience, and their willingness to confront adversity directly.

Falon, catching Gerald's eye, gave him a curt nod. "That was close," Falon admitted, her voice gruff but steady. "Morack's a nasty piece of work. His magic... it feels different, darker than anything I've encountered before." She ran a hand through her hair, her expression thoughtful. "He's not just powerful; he's... cunning. He anticipated our moves, almost as if he knew what we were going to do before we did it."

Gerald found himself agreeing with Falon's assessment. He'd sensed it too – a chilling premonition, a sense of impending doom that had hung heavy in the air before the clash. It wasn't a simple precognitive vision, but an awareness of the currents of dark magic, a sense of the sorcerer's strategy, almost a perception of Morack's intent. This intuitive grasp of the magical currents was a direct result of his own burgeoning powers.

"He'll be back," Elara stated, her voice low and serious. She looked up from the sphere, her eyes reflecting the faint light emanating from its fractured surface. "I can sense it. His magic is tenacious and resilient. This wasn't a defeat; it was a temporary retreat." Finn nodded grimly. "He'll regroup, consolidate his power, and return stronger than before. We need to prepare ourselves." She said, pushing herself away from the stalagmite, her movements deliberate despite her exhaustion. "We need to return to the Sanctury with the crystalline stone and make sure it is safe."

Falon, loudly, interjected, "So it cannot connect with the Serpent's Eye, right? His magic is potent, and his defenses were formidable. We barely managed to push him back. A frontal assault would be suicidal."

Gerald, emboldened by his recent understanding of his own latent abilities, felt a surge of confidence. He knew that his role wasn't just to record the events unfolding around him; it was to actively influence them, to shape the narrative and ensure the survival of Coron. He stepped forward, his notebook clutched in his hand.

"So, we should try to locate the Serpent's Eye," Gerald stated, his voice surprisingly firm and clear. To stop the joining of the crystalline stone and the Serpent's Eye to Morack's dark magic the ultimate power.

Falon listened intently, her initial skepticism slowly giving way to fascination. She had witnessed Gerald's abilities firsthand, the way his words had seemed to bolster their resolve, to bolster their courage, and even to lessen Morack's intensity. She understood that Gerald possessed a unique kind of power, one that complemented their own skills and offered a different path to victory.

"So, you're saying... you can use your words to fight?" Falon asked, her voice filled with a mixture of wonder and apprehension.

Gerald nodded. "I believe so. It's not the brute force of an axe, or the raw power of a spell, but it's a power, nonetheless. It's the power of narrative, the power of story, the power to shape reality itself."

Elara and Finn exchanged knowing glances. They had sensed the shift in Gerald, the awakening of his dormant powers. They knew that this unexpected ally was proving to be a strong weapon in their fight against Morack.

"We need a plan," Elara declared, her voice regaining its strength. "A plan that leverages all of our skills, that utilizes Gerald's abilities to their full potential."

The four of them huddled together, their combined knowledge and skills forming a formidable team. They spent the next few hours meticulously crafting their strategy. They analyzed Morack's tactics after their clash with the sorcerer, identified his weaknesses, and developed a counterstrategy designed to exploit them. Gerald, armed with his notebook and his newfound abilities, would create diversions, dispel illusions, and manipulate the very fabric of reality to give them the upper hand next time they engaged Morack. The cavern, once a throbbing heart of darkness, now lay still, the shattered remnants of Morack's ritual scattered like broken teeth across the floor.

Aldar's shadow still loomed forebodingly, his grip on Coron tightening with each passing moment. Morack's slight defeat was a significant blow, but it was merely a setback, a temporary reprieve in the larger conflict. The battle had revealed the depth of Aldar's power, the extent of his reach, and the insidious nature of his control. The mission gave a sobering awareness of the perilous battle that still lay before them.

The retreat to the Sanctuary of Lost Souls in Coron was a slow, arduous journey. Falon, despite Elara's healing, moved with a pronounced limp, her movements hampered by pain. Finn, too, showed the strain of the battle, his steps hesitant and his breathing labored. Gerald, despite his exhaustion, precisely documented their experiences, his words capturing the raw emotions.

Upon arriving at Sanctuary, they were met with worried faces. The keepers, alerted by Elara's advance warning, were waiting, their concern apparent on their faces. The sight of Falon's injury and Finn's exhaustion confirmed their fears and the weakening of Elara's powers as Mage were interwoven with the anxiety about their injuries, in anticipation of what lay ahead. They recounted to those gathered, in detail of the clash and retrieval of the Heart of Coron stone from Morack.

Elara would create a magical spell to conceal the stone from Morak and Aldar's clutches. They could not take the chance of placing it back in the center of Old Coron, to only have Morack obtain it again.

The coming days were spent in recovery, planning, and preparing for the inevitable confrontation with Aldar's forces. Falon's injury, though severe, was not fatal, and with Elara's tireless care, she slowly began to heal. Finn, with time and rest, slowly regained his fighting strength. Gerald, meanwhile, continued to analyze their experiences, his observations providing critical insights into Aldar's strategies, weaknesses, and the vulnerabilities in his dark magic.

The success of their first battle with Morack had been a turning point, a crucial step in their larger struggle. In the quiet moments of recovery, they found a renewed sense of purpose, a strengthened resolve, and a shared commitment to their cause, a fragile beacon of hope in a Kingdom shrouded in shadow.

11

Aldar's Final Assault

The days that followed were a whirlwind of activity, a frantic dance between preparation and the gnawing dread of the inevitable. The Sanctuary, usually a haven of quiet contemplation, pulsed with an energetic energy. The atmosphere resonated with the mystique of magical preparations, the clanging of steel as weapons were sharpened, and the hushed whispers of fighters devising battle plans. The quiet moments of recovery had been crucial, allowing them to heal both physically and emotionally, to confront the losses they had suffered and steel themselves for the battles to come.

Falon, though still limping, was her boisterous self, her spirits buoyed by Elara's healing and the camaraderie of her cohorts. She spent hours sharpening her axe, the metronomic ring of metal striking metal, a stark contrast to the anxious whispers circulating through the sanctuary. Her laughter, though less frequent than before, carried a newfound depth, a resilience forged in the rigors of their recent battle. She had stared death in the face and survived. This knowledge imbued her with a fierce, unwavering determination.

Finn, his face regaining its customary acuity, worked tirelessly, his mighty sword humming with renewed power. He spent countless hours poring over ancient texts, consulting with the sanctuary's keepers, seeking any advantage, any clue that might tilt the odds in their favor. The strain of the previous clash with Morack was still engrained on his face, the lines around his eyes deeper, his movements slightly slower, but his mind was sharp, his resolve unshakeable. He was a grand player in their defense, the anchor that held the fighters together, and his unwavering focus was a source of strength for all who observed him. Gerald found his role shifting. While his storytelling had proved invaluable, he was now also invaluable as a strategist. His analysis of Morack's tactics, coupled with his keen observation of Aldar's previous actions, revealed patterns, weaknesses, and vulnerabilities. He found himself sketching diagrams on scraps of parchment, plotting strategies, and contributing insights no one else perceived. His analytical mind, sharpened by the pressures of his unexpected situation, was becoming an indispensable asset in their fight for survival.

The gathering of forces was a somber affair. Word of Morack's first defeat, though celebrated, had also spread the grim reality of the threat posed by Aldar. Then there was the Serpent's Eye that had not been found or seen by anyone. Some Coronians were questioning where it was, did Aldar still possess it? Did Morack hide it? Gerald had mentioned, Morack did not have it in the Cavern.

From the far corners of Coron, warriors, mages, and even simple farmers, armed with whatever weapons they could muster, began to arrive at the Sanctuary. They came from villages that had been ravaged by Aldar's forces, from towns that stood on the brink of destruction, from families who had lost loved ones. Everyone carried their own burden, their own grief, their own fierce determination to fight for what was left of their home.

Their ranks were diverse. Towering giants from the northern mountains, their movements graceful despite their size, stood shoulder to shoulder with nimble elves, their archery skills legendary, and the hardy dwarves, renowned for their unmatched resilience and their unwavering loyalty. Humans, from different walks of life seasoned knights, nimble rogues, and powerful mages added their strength to the growing army. Each warrior carried the weight of their homeland, their resolve hardened by the prospect of imminent danger and the lingering memory of recent losses.

Among them were the few remaining members of the Royal Guard, their armor bearing the scars of countless battles, their faces etched with weariness and resoluteness. They were a hardened brotherhood, bound by a shared sense of duty and a profound loyalty to their kingdom. Their presence, though few in number, injected a potent dose of strength and hope into the assembled forces. Their experience and leadership were critical, providing a crucial framework for organizing and strategizing. They carried the weight of their past victories and defeats, a silent testament to their resilience. This fusion of strength and resilience, of determination and despair, painted a poignant image, a testament to the tenacity of the people of Coron.

Once tranquil and isolated, the Coron had become a lively hub of military activity. Armor rattled through the grounds, mingling with the shouted commands of training drills and the soft hum of prayers and spells. A charge of magical energy filled the air, embodying the group's shared resolve and optimism.

Elara worked tirelessly, tending to injuries, mending wounds, and bolstering spirits. Her gentle touch and soothing words provided a much-needed respite from the palpable tension. She moved amongst the warriors, a beacon of hope, weaving her magic into the fabric of their collective resolve.

The days leading up to the final assault were a blur of activity, the children and heavily wounded were moved to a safe chamber in the Sanctuary, Strategies were refined, weapons were sharpened, and spirits were bolstered. Gerald, using his detailed observations and analysis, created an intricate map of Aldar's forces, highlighting potential weaknesses and outlining possible attack routes. This map, along with his insights into Aldar's magical abilities, contributed invaluable intelligence to Finn, who then devised a counterstrategy, designed to disrupt Aldar's magical defenses. The plan was intricate and risky, but it held the potential to turn the tide of the war.

The night before the final assault was a night of quiet preparation. A heavy silence descended upon the Sanctuary, broken only by the occasional rustle of armor or the soft chats of a prayer. Each warrior spent the hours preparing themselves mentally and physically, confronting their fears and accepting the potential for loss. Gerald, amidst the quiet intensity, found himself reflecting on the incredible journey that had brought him to this point. He, a writer grappling with his own creative block, was now standing on the precipice of a decisive battle, his unique skills proving crucial in the fight for a kingdom he had never imagined.

He looked around at the assembled forces, at the determined faces of the Coronians, and felt a profound sense of awe and gratitude. His connection with these people who had become his family. His journey had been extraordinary, a testament to the power of belief, the resilience, and the unexpected ways in which even the most ordinary individuals can find extraordinary strength. He knew the battle that lay ahead would be perilous and potentially fatal, but he also knew that he would face it with courage and staunch resolve. The Kingdom's fate, and his own unexpected destiny, hung precariously in the balance. The final assault was imminent; they prepared to confront Aldar and his legions.

As dawn painted the eastern sky with streaks of fiery orange and dark clouds of smoke, a hush fell over the assembled forces. The nervous energy of the previous days had given way to a quiet intensity, an unmistakable sense of anticipation that hung in the air. The diverse ranks of Coron's defenders stood shoulder to shoulder, a testament to the unity and shared bravery. Giants and elves, dwarves and humans, mages and knights, all differences were set aside, each of their individual strengths merging into a formidable whole. The once disparate elements, each with their own unique traditions and customs, had found common ground in the face of a common enemy.

This unity wasn't merely a tactical arrangement; it was a profound shift in the very spirit of Coron. The shared experience of near destruction, the collective grief over losses suffered, and the desperate hope for survival had woven an unbreakable bond between these people. They were no longer separate factions; they were a single entity, their hearts beating as one, their spirits intertwined in a shared purpose. Even the lingering animosity between some groups, a legacy of past conflicts, had faded in the face of the imminent threat. The old rivalries paled in comparison to the overwhelming need for collective action. Their shared objective had eclipsed all else.

Gerald, observing the scene from a vantage point overlooking the assembled army, felt a surge of pride and admiration. He had witnessed firsthand the transformative power of shared adversity, the way in which a common enemy could forge unexpected alliances and inspire extra ordinary acts of courage. He saw the determination in the eyes of the warriors; he knew that they were ready to brave whatever Aldar threw at them. Their differences, once sources of conflict, had become their strength, a tapestry of skills, abilities, and fighting styles that would prove invaluable in the battle ahead.

The dwarves, noted for their resilience and formidable strength, formed the leading line, their axes reflecting the morning light as they maintained an organized and solid formation. Their reputation for loyalty and dependability provided reassurance in a volatile battle about to unfold. The elves, renowned for their exceptional skills in archery, took positions at elevated vantage points, moving efficiently and quietly to prepare for a coordinated volley of arrows. Their accuracy and effectiveness were well-established, enabling them to strike targets at considerable distances with precision.

The giants, their immense size and strength making them formidable adversaries, acted as the bulwark of the line, forming an impenetrable shield against Aldar's charging forces. Their very presence was a deterrent, their formidable strength able to withstand the brutal onslaught that was sure to come. The humans, a diverse group of warriors from various walks of life, filled the gaps in the line, their experience and adaptability providing the flexibility needed to respond to unexpected challenges. Their versatility was a crucial asset, their ability to adapt to changing battlefield conditions making them a powerful and unpredictable force.

Amongst them moved the Royal Guard, their armor gleaming despite its scars, their faces hardened by years of battles, yet imbued with a quiet confidence that reflected their steadfast loyalty to their kingdom. They were the heart of the defense, their expertise in battle tactics and strategy acting as a crucial backbone for the upcoming battle. Their experience was invaluable, and their presence offered a needed steadiness that soothed the anxieties of the less experienced warriors. Their guidance and training were pivotal, ensuring that the varied forces worked in unison and coordination to be an effective combat force.

Finn, with his sword glowing a nebulous magical energy, moved amongst the ranks, imparting last minute instructions and offering words of encouragement. His calm presence instilled a sense of order and confidence, his quiet authority easily commanding respect and obedience. His voice woven throughout their ranks meant to boost their morale, preparing them both physically and mentally for the daunting task ahead. He was their leader, their guiding light in the storm, a source of inspiration.

Elara's eyes radiating, determined kindness, moved among the soldiers, her healing magic bringing comfort and fresh energy. Her gentle touch eased both wounds and worries, that bound the army together. Giving the Coronians enough courage to face an enemy of great force.

Gerald, despite his initial apprehension, found himself settling into his role as strategist and observer. He had meticulously analyzed Aldar's tactics and identified potential weaknesses in the sorcerer's defenses. He relayed this information to Finn, who, in turn, incorporated it into their overall strategy, tailoring their defensive strategies.

The atmosphere crackled with anticipation, a mixture of fear and exhilaration. This was it. The final battle. The fate of Coron's imminent battle. They had chosen to fight, together, not as separate armies or factions, but as one united force.

The first wave of Aldar's army crashed against Coron's defenses like a tidal wave of darkness. Minotaur's, their horns gleaming wickedly, charged at the dwarven vanguard, their roars shaking the very ground. The dwarves, undeterred, met them head on, their axes biting deep into the monstrous hides, cleaving through bone and muscle with terrifying efficiency. The air filled with the clang of steel on horn, the guttural roars of the beasts, and the battle cries of the dwarves, their voices a furious chorus of defiance.

Simultaneously, a hail of dark sorcery rained down from the sky, launched by Morack, along with his shadowy Mages. Aldar was in position on a nearby hillside observing the attack on Coron with the Serpent's Eye hung around his neck. Spells of chilling ice and searing fire erupted across the battlefield, seeking out gaps in Coron's defenses. The elves, nimble and quick, responded with a barrage of arrows, each shot guided by an almost supernatural precision, finding its mark with deadly accuracy. Their arrows, tipped with enchanted steel, pierced through the ranks of Aldar's undead creatures and their monstrous minions, disrupting the flow of dark magic and forcing them to take cover.

The giants, immovable objects in the path of the encroaching horde, held their ground with unwavering resolve. Their colossal forms, shrouded in shimmering runes of protection, deflected the worst of the onslaught. They stood as barriers, bearing the brunt of the enemy's attacks, their roars echoing across the battlefield. Their immense strength prevented the enemy from breaking through the lines, and their very presence provided a morale boost to the surrounding troops.

Gerald, watching from his vantage point, felt a knot tighten in his stomach. This was far more brutal than he had anticipated, a maelstrom of violence and chaos that threatened to overwhelm even Coron's valiant defenses. He observed the human soldiers, their resilience and adaptability truly remarkable; they were flexible, adjusting their tactics quickly as they moved from one combat situation to another. Their versatility was their strength, their ability to maneuver and react quickly to any changes on the field of battle, allowing them to cover critical ground and adjust their strategy.

The Royal Guard, a steel wall of experience and discipline, moved between the ranks, their swords a blur of motion, their expertise in battle tactics ensuring a cohesive and organized response to the enemy's diverse attacks. Their presence was a constant source of stability in the shifting chaos of battle. Their years of experience guided them through the onslaught, their movements fluid, their tactics flawless. Their training was more than just the art of war; it was a legacy of protecting the kingdom from threats. They were both a force and a shield for the rest of the army.

Finn, his sword crackling with energy, fought side by side with the troops, reinforcing their strength and bolstering their spirits. Elara's spells wove a protective barrier around Coron's lines, weakening Aldar's attacks and enhancing the capabilities of Coron's soldiers. She moved from one position to another, reinforcing the defense with quick, precisely placed spells.

Elara, a whirlwind of healing and compassion, flitted across the battlefield, mending wounds and reviving the fallen. She moved through the troops with calm efficiency that contrasted with the chaos of the battle. Every touch was a blessing, healing the physical wounds and restoring the morale amongst the fighters.

The battle raged for hours, a brutal dance of death and destruction. The ground ran red with blood, the air thick with the stench of sweat, fear, and the acrid smell of burning magic. Yet, Coron's defenders held firm, their unity and resolve unwavering. They fought not only for their kingdom but for their homes, their families, and their very survival. As the hours wore on, the exhaustion and despair began to set in, but their morale remained intact, fueled by the shared belief that they were fighting not just for themselves, but for their land.

As the sun began to set, casting long, ominous shadows across the battlefield, Gerald noticed a change in Aldar's tactics. Morack was without the Heart of Coron, or the crystalline stone, so he was unable to complete the ritual with the Serpent's Eye that Aldar possessed.

The relentless assault began to lose its intensity, replaced by a more methodical approach. He realized that Aldar was trying to tire out the Coron forces, to wear down their defenses before launching a final, decisive strike. He quickly relayed this observation to Finn, who immediately adjusted the Coronian strategy, shifting from a purely defensive posture to one of calculated counteroffensives.

The change in tactics proved crucial. Energized by the shift and Elara's magic, the Coronians launched coordinated attacks that disrupted and repelled his forces. The dwarves, with renewed ferocity, broke through the enemy's line, creating a pathway for the elves to rain down a devastating volley of arrows. The giants, their power undiminished, held their position, smashing the weakened enemy, pushing them into disarray. The humans, nimble and adaptive, seized the opportunities presented by the disarray, striking with precision and cunning, forcing the enemy to withdraw and retreat.

As the first rays of dawn broke the horizon, illuminating the blood-soaked battlefield, it became clear that the tide had turned. Aldar's army, battered, broken, and demoralized, began a disorganized retreat. Morack, his face contorted with fury, made a desperate attempt to regroup his forces, unleashing a final barrage of dark magic, but it was too late. Reports from the battlefield had mentioned that Morack was retreating. That was good news to the Coronians, a devasting blow to Aldar's intention of opening a gateway to other realms. Aldar had not been seen, nor the Serpent's Eye.

The combined might of Coron had proven too formidable, its unity and resilience unshakeable. His forces, unable to withstand the sustained onslaught, began a hasty retreat.

Many brave souls had fallen in the defense of Coron, their sacrifice a testament to their unwavering loyalty and courage. But they had prevailed, pushing back the darkness, defending their kingdom from the clutches of Aldar and saving Coron from utter annihilation. As the sun rose, casting its golden light upon the battered, but victorious, defenders of Coron, a sense of profound relief and triumph washed over the land. The echoes of the battle would forever reverberate through the land, a stark reminder of the price of freedom and the enduring power of unity against overwhelming odds.

The retreating army left behind a trail of carnage, a grim testament to the ferocity of the battle. Coron's victory was undeniable, yet there were many losses. Gerald, amidst the silent aftermath, felt a profound sense of emptiness, a hollow ache that resonated deeper than the physical exhaustion that weighed upon him. He had witnessed the brutal efficiency of Aldar's forces, their ruthless disregard for life. He'd seen the courage of Coron's defenders, their unwavering spirit in the face of overwhelming odds. He'd participated, albeit indirectly, in the victory, but a nagging feeling persisted a sense that something more was required, a deeper sacrifice, was needed to ensure Coron's future.

His gaze fell upon the shattered remnants of a siege weapon, a massive catapult, its wooden frame splintered and charred, a grotesque parody of its former destructive power. An idea, audacious and perilous, began to form in his mind, a desperate gamble born out of a grim assessment of the situation. The victory was fragile, a temporary reprieve, not a decisive end. Aldar's forces, dwindling but not defeated, could easily regroup and return with a greater, more ferocious army. Coron was still vulnerable. The defenses, although holding, were weakened and battered. More importantly, there was a lingering, insidious threat, Morack. The sorcerer's dark magic, though momentarily disrupted, remained a significant danger, a constant looming threat that could undermine the future of Coron.

Gerald knew he couldn't fight directly. His strengths lay not in swordplay or magic, but in his understanding of strategy and his ability to analyze patterns. He looked at the scattered remains of Aldar's forces, weapons, armor, and the lingering scent of dark magic. It wasn't a physical battle he could win; it was a battle of intellect, of strategic thinking. He had an unconventional weapon, one that was far more potent than any sword or spell. He had his writing. His talent, his gift, seemed insignificant compared to the raw power displayed on the battlefield, but he knew it could be a game changer in this conflict.

His plan was daring, bordering on suicidal, but he felt a strange sense of clarity, a certainty that this was his path. He decided to use his unique abilities to exploit a critical weakness in Aldar's strategy: his reliance on Morack and his dark magic. Morack was the engine of Aldar's destructive power, the source of his relentless assaults. If Morack could be neutralized, Aldar's ability to wage war would be crippled. Gerald wouldn't face Morack in a magical duel; his weapon was far more subtle, far more insidious: a story.

He gathered materials – scraps of parchment, charred remnants of Aldar's siege weapons, even some bits of cloth from fallen soldiers' uniforms. He began to write, the rhythmic scratching of his quill a stark contrast to the desolate silence of the battlefield.

His narrative was a psychological weapon, meticulously crafted to exploit Morack's weaknesses, his ego, his desperate need for validation. He painted a picture of Morack as a tragically flawed figure, highlighting the bitter regrets and lingering doubts that haunted his existence.

Days turned into nights. He wrote relentlessly, fueled by a strange blend of determination and dread. He worked feverishly, his words taking on a life of their own, as he wove a tale that could cripple an army. He didn't sleep, driven by an inner urgency, a deep knowledge that time was of the essence. His fingers were raw and bleeding, his eyes bloodshot and burning, but he continued writing, his dedication unwavering, his purpose clear.

Finally, the story was complete. It was a long, intricate narrative, designed to resonate on multiple levels, its magic working through subtle suggestions and psychological manipulation, rather than overt spells and incantations. Gerald penned his writings on the ancient parchment, scribed to look as though they were a prophecy written many millennia ago. He believed that Morack would accept the writing to be true because of his inability to forge the ritual, he had neither the Heart of Coron crystalline stone or the Serpent's Eye that had disappeared along with Aldar. His loss of previous battles, including the one in the cavern. Gerald also scribed how the destructive force of dark magic had consumed Morack, his downfall being inevitable. His scribed story, a subtle but potent weapon, was poised to change the course of the future, ensuring the lasting peace of a King-dom.

He placed one copy of the manuscript in the Sanctuary, a fragile scrolled filled with his painstakingly written tale, entrusting a second copy to Finn, who agreed to deliver it discreetly to Morak, under the guise of a captured spy. Gerald knew the risks. His plan was a dangerous gamble, one that could cost Finn his life. But he believed it was the only chance to ensure Coron's survival.

The silence following Finn's departure was deafening. The battlefield, even days after the clash, still reeked of smoke and burnt blood. The air, thick with the lingering odor of dark magic, clung to Gerald like a shroud. He sat amidst the wreckage, the weight of his actions pressing down on him like a physical burden. He had gambled every-thing on a single, audacious plan, a desperate attempt to circumvent another direct confrontation with Aldar's for-midable forces vanquishing Morak's powers.

News trickled in from the outposts, fragmented reports of Aldar's movements, rumors of his armies dwindling. Waiting on Aldar's next incursion or maneuver or offen-sive, was more agonizing with each passing day.

Then, one crisp morning, a raven arrived, its feathers ruffled, its demeanor urgent. It bore a message, a single, tightly rolled scroll tied with a black ribbon. A wave of icy dread washed over Gerald, his heart pounding in his chest. This was it. The moment of truth. The answer to his auda-cious gambling.

Elara, visibly concern methodically opened the scroll. The content was succinct and impersonal. It indicated that Morack was incapacitated, his magical abilities rendered ineffective, and his power appeared to have dissipated. No additional information or clarification was provided. The communication was limited to a factual statement, directly acknowledging a defeat. There was no mention regarding the status of Aldar.

A collective gasp escaped the gathered Coronians. The news spread like wildfire, igniting a spark of hope in the hearts of the weary. The weight of uncertainty that had been crushing them lifted slightly, replaced by a fragile sense of relief. But the victory felt incomplete, hollow, tainted by the immense losses suffered during the siege. The cost of their survival was profound.

The city was in ruins, its people maimed and battered from battle, its defenses decimated. Gerald words had won the battle, but they hadn't healed the wounds of war. He had used his unique abilities to achieve a strategic victory, but the emotional and physical scars of the conflict would take far longer to mend. He saw the faces of the mourners, etched with grief and loss. He saw the empty stares of the survivors, haunted by the horrors they had witnessed. The revelation was both unsettling and profoundly validating. He had used the art of fiction, his very life's work, as a weapon of war. His writing, once perceived as a solitary pursuit, had proven to be a force to be reckoned with, a formidable power in the face of unimaginable darkness.

12

Rebuilding Coron

The sun, a pale disc in the smoke filled sky, cast long, skeletal shadows across the ravaged landscape of Coron. The air, once vibrant with the sounds of life, now echoed with the mournful cries of ravens circling the piles of rubble that were once homes. The stench of decay, a macabre perfume, hung heavy, a constant reminder of the brutal battle that had reshaped their Kingdom. The battle, won and dearly purchased, felt hollow amidst the devastation. This wasn't the triumphant return the Coronians had envisioned; this was a grim homecoming to a city reduced to ashes.

Gerald, his clothes torn and stained, moved through the streets, or what remained of them. His boots crunched on broken glass and shattered stone, the sounds a grim counterpoint to the quiet sobs that emanated from the makeshift shelters constructed from salvaged timbers and tattered fabrics. The faces he saw were carved with grief, with the indelible marks of trauma. Children, their eyes wide with a fear far beyond their years, clutched at their parents' ragged clothing, their small bodies still trembling in the chilled air.

The scale of the destruction was overwhelming. Entire districts were leveled, reduced to smoldering heaps of debris. The magnificent Coronian Palace, once a symbol of pride and power, was now a in ruin, its majestic spires broken and blackened, a testament to the ferocity of Aldar's assault. The market square, once bustling with life, was now a desolate expanse, littered with the debris of shattered stalls and broken wares. The very heart of Coron had been ripped apart.

Rebuilding Coron wouldn't happen in just a few days or weeks; instead, it would be an immense challenge that would push the city's resources and resilience to their breaking points. The top priorities were obvious: offering shelter and meals to those displaced, caring for the wounded, and ensuring proper burials for the deceased. With damaged infrastructure, polluted water sources, and broken communication lines, the community faced enormous obstacles—an uphill battle that at times seemed daunting impossible to overcome.

Yet, amidst the despair, a flicker of hope emerged. The Coronians, battered but not broken, began to organize, to rally around the shared goal of rebuilding their shattered city. They worked tirelessly, fueled by a potent mix of grief, determination, and a stubborn refusal to surrender to despair.

Gerald found himself working alongside them, his own physical and emotional wounds aching in sympathy with theirs. His role, initially one of a reluctant warrior, now shifted towards that of a quiet, steadfast leader. He helped to clear the rubble, his hands raw and bleeding, his body aching with exhaustion. He helped to distribute food and water, comforting the grieving and offering words of encouragement to the weary. He listened to the stories of loss and survival, absorbing the tapestry of human resilience that was being woven amidst the ruins. He became a conduit for their collective grief and shared their hope for a brighter future.

Falon, indefatigable, proved to be an invaluable asset in the rebuilding efforts. Her knowledge of engineering and construction, coupled with her tireless energy, helped to organize the chaotic task of clearing debris and constructing temporary shelters. Her jovial spirit, seemingly fazed by the devastation, infused the recovery effort with a much needed dose of levity and optimism.

Elara, her quiet wisdom a soothing balm amidst the chaos, tended to the spiritual wounds of the city. She provided solace to the grieving, offering comfort and counsel to those struggling to cope with their loss. She also played a crucial role in coordinating the efforts to restore the city's magical defenses, a task that would prove to be both crucial and challenging. The Sanctuary of Lost Souls became a haven, a sanctuary for both the living and the spirits of those lost in the battle.

The task of rebuilding Coron wasn't limited to physical reconstruction. The city's social fabric had been severely damaged, requiring painstaking efforts to mend the wounds of war. Trust had been shattered, suspicion festered, and deep divisions emerged amongst the survivors. Gerald recognized the need for unity and healing and actively sought to bridge the chasm of mistrust that threatened to divide them. His stories, carefully crafted to reflect the shared experience of loss and triumph, became a unifying force, reminding them of their shared heritage and their common goal of rebuilding their lives and their city.

Slowly, gradually, Coron began to rise from the ashes. New shelters emerged from the debris, their roughhewn walls rising like defiant symbols of hope. The streets, though still scared, were slowly being cleared, the rubble being transformed into foundations for a new beginning.

But the scars of war remained, indelible marks on the landscape and the souls of its inhabitants. The rebuilding efforts were far from complete; many challenges remained. The economic fallout of the war, the trauma sustained by the survivors, and the seated anxieties about Aldar's potential return all created a complex and fragile environment.

Gerald's influence, through his command of narrative, continued to exert significant impact—shaping not only the city's physical recovery but also strengthening its communal resolve. Although the future remained uncertain, the citizens of Coron expressed gratitude to Gerald Weaver, their unexpected hero, and prepared to confront forthcoming challenges together. Despite extensive devastation, their city was showing signs of revival. The echoes of conflict gradually diminished, Giving way to sounds of construction reverberating throughout the city

One of the initial steps in the recovery process was the burial of the deceased. Numerous bodies were scattered throughout the ruins, their final locations reflecting the disorder and destruction of the city. Falon, maintaining a positive disposition, demonstrated resolute commitment as she coordinated groups to respectfully retrieve and prepare those who fell. Elara conducted rites of passage, ensuring that the souls of those lost received appropriate guidance. The environment was permeated by incense and solemnity, with mournful chants resonating through the devastated city, providing a measured response to the tragedy.

Much care and attention was vital to heal the survivors. Despite sustaining damage, the Sanctuary functioned as an improvised hospital. Teams of healers, combining expertise in traditional medicine with ancient healing practices of Coron, worked diligently to care for the injured. Procedures included the setting of fractures, cleaning and bandaging of wounds, and attentive care for the ill provided with deep empathy. Gerald contributed as needed, offering supportive remarks and recounting stories to help sooth distress. His narratives, originating from a former life now distant, offered brief relief from the demanding circumstances faced by those under their care.

Food and water supplies were limited. The city's wells had become contaminated, and the nearby farmland, formerly a key food source, was severely damaged. Falon applied her engineering expertise in collaboration with others to purify available water sources, constructing basic filtration and purification systems from salvaged materials. Although the task was highly demanding, her perseverance contributed significantly to maintaining group morale.

The rebuilding itself began tentatively, amidst the rubble and despair. The Coronians, initially dazed and overwhelmed, began to find their purpose. The shared grief bonded them, forging a stronger sense of community than ever before. The process of reconstructing the Palace was particularly challenging. Its central tower, once a symbol of the kingdom's might, had been reduced to a crumbling skeleton. Engineers and mages worked side by side, employing ancient techniques and innovative magic to stabilize the structure, painstakingly repairing and reinforcing its shattered foundations. The work progressed slowly, but each stone replaced, each beam reinforced, was a symbol of the Coronians' true bravery.

The market square, once a vibrant hub of activity, was now a desolate courtyard. Yet, even here, the seeds of recovery were sown. Small stalls, fashioned from salvaged materials, began to spring up, offering a limited selection of goods. Bartering and trade, once formalized and regulated, became a spontaneous act of mutual support. This blossoming market, far from polished or organized, was a powerful testament to the resilience of the Coronians. It was a symbol of their return to normalcy, a fragile reminder of a life that was slowly being reclaimed.

Gerald, drawing upon his knowledge of human psychology, offered a different kind of comfort. He listened to their stories, validating their experiences and helping them to find meaning in their pain. He helped them articulate their losses, channeling their grief into a creative process that began to heal and transform. He encouraged them to share their experiences through art, music, and stories, a way to collectively process their trauma and build a shared narrative of resilience.

The children, in particular, bore the weight of the tragedy. They had witnessed horrors beyond their comprehension. Gerald, recognizing their particular needs, initiated storytelling sessions, creating magical narratives that offered them escape and comfort. He wove tales of bravery, friendship, and hope, transporting them to worlds where good ultimately triumphed over evil. These storytelling sessions became a vital part of the healing process, allowing children to process their fear and begin to rebuild their sense of safety and security.

The weeks turned into months, and the months into a year. Coron slowly began to resemble a city again. The rebuilt sections, though modest, displayed a sense of renewed purpose. The architecture, while blending the old and the new, reflected a growing confidence. New homes were built alongside the repaired ones, their colors echoing the resilience of the Coronians, a vibrant testament to their struggle for survival. The air, still tinged with the lingering scent of smoke and ash, now carried the fresh aroma of newly planted flowers and herbs. It was a city that was not merely being rebuilt, but was being reimagined, reshaped by the crucible of conflict.

The journey was far from over, but Coron, under the unlikely guidance of a writer from another world, was well on its way to recovery, stronger, and more resilient than before. The future remained uncertain, but the city, its inhabitants, and their unlikely champion were ready to face it, together.

The Sanctuary of Lost Souls, though itself damaged, became a makeshift mortuary. Within its hallowed halls, where lost souls once sought solace, now lay the bodies of Coron's heroes. The wounded were cared for in one wing, their moans and gasps a stark counterpoint to the quiet dignity of the fallen in the adjacent chambers.

Gerald, initially overwhelmed by the scale of the tragedy, found himself strangely drawn to the task. He learned the names of those lost, not just as statistics on a battlefield, but as individuals with stories, families, and dreams. He listened to their loved ones recount their lives, their laughter, their ambitions, and their fears. He absorbed their tales, recognizing the profound significance of chronicling these lives to ensure their memory wouldn't fade amidst the wreckage of the city.

The actual burial process became a ritual, a collective act of remembrance. A vast trench was dug outside the city walls, its scale a grim testament to the losses suffered. As each body was gently lowered into the earth. The Coronians gathered, each carrying a single flower or a piece of stone to lay upon the earth, a silent offering of respect. Lyra delivered a moving eulogy, her words simple yet powerful, acknowledging each victim by name, recognizing their sacrifice, and honoring their memory.

Gerald, watching this solemn act, felt a profound sense of connection to these people he had only recently come to know. These were not just names in a history book, but real individuals who had fought and died for their home. Their sacrifice was not in vain, a testament to the enduring spirit of Coron, a foundation upon which the city would be rebuilt.

The city's artisans, whose lives had been spared, created simple headstones from salvaged materials. They etched names, ages, and brief epitaphs onto the stone, capturing snippets of the lost lives in a way that was both poignant and deeply personal. The headstones were small, simple, yet each one represented a life lived, a story cut tragically short. They were a poignant reminder that Coron had survived, but at a profound cost.

In the days that followed, memorial services were held throughout the city, each one unique, mirroring the diverse culture of Coron. Some were solemn affairs, steeped in tradition, with mournful chants and prayers. Others were joyous celebrations of life, filled with music, stories, and laughter, remembering the fallen with the vibrancy that defined their lives.

Even the children participated, each in their own way. The children's art adorned the walls of the Sanctuary, colorful yet melancholic paintings reflecting their sorrow yet exhibiting their indomitable spirit. Their art became a testament to their resilience, a bridge between grief and the hope for a better future.

The memory of the fallen wasn't just a somber ritual; it was a transformative process, a necessary step on Coron's path to healing. It was a powerful demonstration of the unwavering spirit of Coron, a city reborn from the ashes of conflict, forever shaped by the memory of its heroes. The scars of battle would remain, a constant reminder of the price of freedom, but so would the memory of those who paid the ultimate price – a memory that would fuel the city's rebuilding, ensuring that their sacrifice would never be forgotten. The city, now bearing the weight of profound grief and the resolve to move forward, was ready to face the immense challenge of reconstruction.

The job of physically rebuilding Coron was daunting, but equally challenging was the reconstruction of its social fabric. The war had not only shattered buildings; it had fractured the very heart of the kingdom. Families were torn apart, livelihoods destroyed, and the established social order thrown into chaos. The familiar rhythm of life, once a comforting cadence, was now a discordant symphony of grief and uncertainty. This was where Gerald, with his unexpected skills and his outsider's perspective, found a new role, one that transcended the simple acts of physical labor he had undertaken earlier.

Falon, established work crews, meticulously assigning tasks based on individuals' skills and abilities. She implemented a system of resource allocation, ensuring that materials were distributed fairly and efficiently. She understood that rebuilding a city was more than just bricks and mortar; it was about rebuilding lives and restoring hope.

Elara, meanwhile, focused on the emotional and spiritual wellbeing of the populace. She established support groups, offering solace and guidance to those struggling with grief and trauma. She organized communal rituals, blending Coronian traditions with her own unique insights, creating ceremonies that offered both comfort and a sense of collective purpose. Her presence was a beacon of hope, radiating calmness amidst the chaos of reconstruction.

Gerald, having witnessed firsthand the devastation and the resilience of the Coronians, discovered a talent for mediation and conflict resolution. He had observed that the very act of sharing stories, of listening and validating each other's experiences, helped mend broken relationships and foster unity.

One of the most pressing issues was the resettlement of displaced families. Many had lost their homes, their livelihoods, and their sense of belonging. Gerald, working closely with Falon and Elara, devised a system that prioritized the most vulnerable, ensuring that those with the greatest needs were provided with immediate shelter and support. They collaborated with local artisans and craftsmen, who had managed to preserve their skills, to repair and reconstruct homes, creating a systematic approach to rebuilding homes while providing employment for the many who were left without work.

The reconstruction of Coron's institutions was equally complex. The city council, previously a bastion of order, had been decimated. New leadership needed to be chosen, and the power dynamics within the city had to be carefully renegotiated. Gerald encouraged collaboration and consensus building, ensuring that the city's government was representative of its diverse population, fostering inclusiveness in all decision making processes.

The rebuilding of Coron's economy was equally challenging. This involved the revitalization of the city's trade networks and the creation of new economic opportunities. They established trade agreements with neighboring regions, ensuring that Coron would once again become a center of commerce. They encouraged innovation and entrepreneurship, providing resources and support to new businesses.

The legal system, too, required urgent attention. There was a danger of chaos and vigilantism. The Coronians knew the importance of the rule of law, they worked to establish a new legal framework, one that was fair, just, and representative of the people of Coron.

Perhaps the most significant challenge was restoring a sense of hope and optimism to the people of Coron. It was a daunting task to restore faith in the future. This is where Elara's work was crucial. Through communal rituals, storytelling, and acts of collective healing, she helped to rekindle a sense of unity and shared purpose.

The rebuilding of Coron was not simply a physical process; it was a social, economic, and spiritual transformation. It was a testament to the perseverance of the Coron's spirit. The process was slow, arduous, and fraught with challenges, but with each stone laid, each home rebuilt, and each community project completed, Coron began to rise again, stronger and more unified than ever before.

The election of the new city council was a momentous occasion, a beacon of hope amidst the rubble and the lingering shadows of war. Instead of bitter infighting and power struggles, there was a surprising consensus. The candidates, representing a diverse range of backgrounds and professions, were chosen not for their lineage or wealth, but for their proven commitment to Coron's wellbeing. Anya, a skilled architect who had tirelessly worked on the rebuilding efforts, was elected as the council's leader. Her pragmatic approach, combined with her unwavering optimism, resonated deeply with the populace. She embodied the spirit of Coron's rebirth, a phoenix rising from the ashes of destruction.

Anya's first act as leader was to establish a council dedicated to long term planning. This wasn't merely about rebuilding what had been lost; it was about creating a better Coron, a city resilient to future threats. The council comprised individuals from various walks of life – farmers, artisans, merchants, and scholars – each contributing their unique perspectives and expertise to the discussions. Gerald, while not a member of the council, served as an advisor, providing insights gleaned from his vastly different world, offering fresh perspectives on governance, resource management, and sustainable development. His unconventional methods sometimes challenged the traditional ways of Coron, but his genuine concern for its people ensured that his suggestions were always met with serious consideration. One of the key initiatives was the establishment of a comprehensive education system. Recognizing that a well-educated populace was the foundation of a strong and prosperous society, Anya's council prioritized the construction of schools and the training of teachers. The curriculum included not only the basics of reading, writing, and arithmetic but also practical skills like agriculture, engineering, and craftsmanship, ensuring that the children of Coron were well prepared to contribute to their city's rebuilding and prosperity.

The revitalization of Coron's economy was another significant undertaking. The council, working in close collaboration with Finn and a team of skilled dwarven engineers, focused on repairing the infrastructure that supported commerce, repairing damaged roads, bridges, and canals, restoring vital transportation links. This improved the flow of goods and people, facilitating trade and bolstering the city's economic recovery. They established fair trade practices, ensuring that merchants and artisans receive equitable compensation for their work. The idea was not just to recreate what had been lost, but to build a more robust and resilient economy, one that was less reliant on single industries and more diversified to withstand future seiges. This forward thinking approach garnered considerable support, and soon, new businesses started springing up, offering a range of goods and services, from clothing and tools to food and entertainment, creating a thriving market that injected life into Coron's streets.

Gerald played a unique role in this process, using his skill as a writer to document the lives and experiences of the Coronians. He collaborated with local artists to create murals and sculptures depicting Coron's history, its struggles, and its enduring spirit. His stories, shared through community gatherings and written down in books, became a source of collective memory and shared identity, reinforcing the sense of community that had been vital to their survival. The narratives became both a record of the past and a source of hope for the future. As months turned into seasons, Coron continued its transformation, shedding its wartorn past and embracing a bright and hopeful future. The rhythm of life, once a discordant symphony, began to return to its former comforting cadence, but now enriched by the resilience, empathy, and newfound unity of its people. Gerald, once an outsider, now considered himself a member of Coron, his life intertwined with the destiny of this vibrant kingdom, forever changed by his role in their rebirth.

13

Gerald's Choice

The scent of woodsmoke and baking bread hung heavy in the crisp Coronian air, a stark contrast to the sterile, predictable aroma of his own apartment back in London. Gerald sat on the edge of the Sanctuary's crumbling stone well, the cool night air chilling his skin. He'd spent weeks immersed in Coron's rebirth, a whirlwind of reconstruction, governance, and storytelling. He'd become an unlikely leader, a bridge between two worlds, a writer who'd found his narrative not in ink on paper, but in the very fabric of a kingdom's resurrection. Yet, the familiar ache of longing tugged at his heart. The decision loomed, a chasm yawning between two lives, two realities. Return to the familiar anxieties of his writer's block and the lonely rhythm of his London existence, or remain in this fantastic and unusual realm, a place he'd saved, a place that had undeniably saved him.

Elara found him there, a silent figure draped in the shadows of the ancient oak. She offered him a steaming mug of something fragrant and spicy, its warmth seeping into his chilled hands. "The whispers of the forest grow louder, Gerald," she said softly, her voice carrying the weight of ancient wisdom. "They speak of your choice, of the path that lies ahead."

He sighed, the sound heavy with the burden of his indecision. "It's not a simple choice, Elara. One life feels like a half-life dream, the other a fantastical reality that's become my new normal." He gestured towards the distant, twinkling lights of Coron, a city rising from the ashes, a testament to the resilience of its people. "I've helped build something incredible here. I've found a purpose, a sense of belonging I never knew existed."

"And yet," Elara continued, her gaze piercing, "the pull of your other world remains. The familiar comforts, the routines, the...absence of magic."

The absence of magic. He hadn't even realized how much he'd come to rely on the subtle enchantment that permeated Coron, the way the very air seemed to flow with energy. The magic was more than just spells and fantastical creatures; it was a fundamental aspect of life, woven into the very fabric of existence, a stark contrast to the reality of his former life. He had witnessed magic heal the sick, strengthen the weak, and unite the divided. Could he truly go back to a world devoid of such wonder?

Falon arrived, her hair dusted with frost. She patted Gerald on the back, her hearty laugh echoing through the quiet night. "Don't fret so, friend! It's not as if you're abandoning us. Your stories will carry Coron with you, wherever you go. Every word you write, every tale you tell, will be a bridge between our worlds."

Gerald smiled, a genuine smile that eased the tension in his chest. Falon's words struck a chord. His writing, once a source of frustration, had become a vital tool in Coron's reconstruction, a means of preserving its history, its struggles, its triumphs. His ability to weave stories, to capture the essence of a people, had been unexpectedly valuable, proving that even in a world of magic, the power of words held immense sway.

Finn, usually reserved, joined them, his eyes carrying a knowing glint. "Remember, the prophecy spoke of a Bridgebinder, Gerald. Not just a physical bridge, but a bridge between worlds, between hearts. You are the Bridgebinder, whether you choose to remain here or return to your world."

The weight of the prophecy pressed down on him again. He was the key, not just to Coron's survival, but to the potential connection between his world and Coron. The implications were staggering. Could he be the harbinger of a new era, a link between seemingly disparate realities? The thought filled him with both excitement and apprehension. What if he could use his skills to bring some of the lessons of Coron—of community, resilience, and the healing power of storytelling—to his own world?

Days turned into weeks as Gerald wrestled with his decision. He spent hours in the Sanctuary's library, poring over ancient texts, searching for more clues and answers. He walked the streets of Coron, observing the city's gradual recovery, feeling a profound connection to its people, a responsibility he couldn't easily shake. He found himself increasingly drawn to the young children, their faces alight with hope and the promise of a brighter future. Their eyes held a spark of magic that reminded him of the vibrant heart of Coron, a vibrant heart he had helped to mend.

He spent countless hours writing, pouring his experiences into his journal, crafting stories that captured the essence of Coron, weaving the magic and wonder into tales that could resonate with readers far away. He wrote about the resilience of the Coronians, their staunch determination in the face of adversity. He chronicled the bravery of their soldiers, the ingenuity of their engineers, the healing touch of their healers. He wrote about Elara's unwavering faith, Finn's quiet strength, and Falon's boisterous optimism. He wrote about Anya's leadership, and the gradual return to normalcy, laced with a newfound appreciation for community and collaboration.

He wrote about his own transformation, the unexpected ways in which he'd found a sense of purpose and belonging in this extraordinary world. He scribed about his struggles, his doubts, and his ultimate decision. He wrote about his the twists and turns of his life.

He realized that his voyage wasn't over but had merely entered a new chapter. Whether he stayed in Coron or returned to his own world, his writing would forever be intertwined with the fate of this magical kingdom, a kingdom that had taught him more about himself, about courage.

Finally, he sat down, quill in hand, and wrote his final entry. He detailed his decision, his reasons, and his hopes for the future. His decision, he realized, wasn't about abandoning one life for another, but about carrying the spirit of Coron with him, wherever he went, using his storytelling to inspire hope and unity in both worlds.

He thought of Elara—her wisdom, strength, and unwavering support. He recalled her concerned eyes during the battle and how she comforted him in his darkest moments. Leaving her and the Sanctuary's peace felt unimaginable.

Then there was Finn, the quiet, stoic keeper of the Sanctuary, whose words were few but always carried the weight of centuries of experience. His support had been a rock, a steady presence during Gerald's emotional turmoil. He'd seen Finn's quiet acts of kindness, the way he'd always make sure Gerald had a warm place to sleep, a comforting meal ready, a space for him to collect his thoughts. The depth of Finn's loyalty was evident in the smallest gestures, through the gaze of his eyes that spoke volumes when words were unnecessary. Leaving him behind felt like betraying a trust built on shared hardship and mutual respect. And Falon, a female dwarf, whose laughter could fill even the darkest corners of the Coron, had become an unexpected friend, a confidante, a source of optimism. Falon's loyalty wasn't just a matter of words; it was evident in her actions. She had risked her life alongside Gerald. He thought of their shared adventures, the dangerous journey through the Black Forest, the nail biting moments during the battle against Aldar's forces – moments that had forged a bond stronger than steel. To leave Falon behind felt like severing a piece of his own heart.

Beyond the keepers of the Sanctuary, there were the people of Coron. He thought of Anya, the courageous leader who had rallied her people, her bold spirit inspiring everyone around her. He remembered the strength in her eyes, the wisdom in her voice, and the way she'd entrusted him with a role he never thought he could fulfill. He'd seen her resilience firsthand, her ability to lift her people's spirits even in the darkest hours, her dedication to rebuilding their city from the ashes. He thought of the children, their bright eyes full of hope, their laughter echoing through the streets of the reborn city. They looked at him with a mixture of awe and affection, seeing him as a symbol of hope and redemption. Walking away from them and giving up on the future they worked so hard to create, felt like betraying their trust and shattering their emerging hopes.

He thought about the artisans, their hands working tirelessly to rebuild their city, their skills creating beauty amidst the destruction. He'd witnessed their dedication, their relentless hope, their refusal to let Aldar extinguish the spark of creativity within them. He'd shared stories with them, listening to their histories, their struggles, their aspirations. Their stories were woven into the very soul of the city, and his writing helped them preserve their memories.

He thought of the soldiers, their faces etched with the scars of battle, yet their determination unyielding. He'd shared their burdens, felt their fear, witnessed their courage. He'd seen their resilience, their commitment to protecting their people, their belief in the possibility of a better future. He'd written about their bravery, their sacrifice, their un-yielding spirit. Leaving their stories, memories, and tri-umphs felt like losing a part of himself. He felt he couldn't tell their stories unless he stayed; their survival and future were bound to his.

Gerald realized that his decision wasn't solely his to make. It was a decision that involved the lives and futures of many.

The bonds of friendship and loyalty he'd formed in Coron were as strong as any magical enchantment, as en-during as the ancient stones of the Sanctuary. They were a testament to the spirit's resilience and the power of con-nection in a world often defined by isolation. These bonds, he realized, were the most potent magic of all. They were the true bridge between worlds, a bridge he could not, and would not, break. The decision, he finally understood, was not a choice between two worlds, but a choice of how to carry the magic of Coron, the spirit of its people, into his own life, regardless of which world he inhabited. His jour-ney had not ended, but was merely transformed into a new chapter, one where his storytelling became the bridge across realities, carrying the hopes and dreams of Coron into his own world, forever changing the narrative of his life.

He carefully considered the significance of his newly dis-covered purpose, which remained consistently present in his thinking. His skills, once perceived as a personal weak-ness – his writer's block, his struggle to find a compelling narrative – were now his greatest strengths. He realized that his words held the power to shape perceptions, inspire courage, and to immortalize the heroism of ordinary individuals. His pen wasn't just an instrument for personal expression; it was a rebirth.

The idea motivated him with a renewed sense of creativity that he had not experienced since his early years, prior to the constraints imposed by expectation which diminished his interest in storytelling. He viewed Coron's stories not as separate accounts of courage, but as related elements within a broader narrative framework.

He envisioned books filled with vivid descriptions of the enchanted landscapes of Coron, the mystical creatures that inhabited their forests, and the magic that pulsed through its very veins. His words could transport readers to a world brimming with wonder, a world worthy of being saved. He imagined the children's tales, woven with elements of magic and courage, tales that would instill hope in the younger generation of Coron, helping them understand the sacrifices of their elders and inspiring them to carry the flame of freedom into the future. He could write about Falon's unwavering loyalty, Finn's quiet strength, and Elara's wisdom, giving voice to the profound relationships that had formed during his time in Coron. These characters, who had become his family, deserved to have their stories told. This new understanding solidified his decision regarding his return.

His choice was no longer a question of choosing between two worlds but a choice of how to bridge them, how to weave the magic of Coron into the fabric of his own life. His stories, his words, would become that Bridgebinder, carrying the experiences of Coron to his own world, transforming the narrative of his life in ways he could scarcely imagine. His writing, once a source of frustration and self-doubt, would now become his greatest weapon, his most powerful magic.

Gerald Weaver, the Bridgebinder, a writer, would write his own destiny, and in doing so, he would document the tales of Coron and it's way of life. And that, he realized, was a story worth telling before returning to his own world.

14

A New Era for a Kingdom

The air crackled with anticipation, an energy that thrummed through the cobbled streets of Coron. For weeks, the city had been abuzz with preparations, a flurry of activity that belied the recent devastation. Artisans, their hands still bearing the marks of their labor rebuilding the shattered city, had meticulously crafted banners and decorations. The scent of baking bread and roasting meats mingled with the fragrance of wildflowers, a poignant reminder of the kingdom's enduring resilience. Children, bright eyes with excitement, chased pigeons through the newly repaired squares, their laughter echoing off the freshly plastered walls. Even the soldiers, their faces etched with the weariness of war, seemed to carry a lightness in their step, a hope that hadn't been present in months.

This was not just a celebration; it was a resurrection. A testament to the staunch spirit of the Coronians, their ability to rise from the ashes of despair and embrace a new dawn. The coronation of a leader, a man who had arrived as a stranger and emerged as a Bridgebinder. Gerald Weaver, the writer who had stumbled into their world, stood poised to receive the kingdoms Royal Honor of Bravery. His selection had not been born of royal lineage or military prowess; it was due to his leadership, his empathy, his strong belief in the people of Coron.

The day dawned clear and bright, the sun painting the sky in hues of gold and rose. Anya, her regal radiating strength and grace, walked alongside Gerald, their presence, a symbol of the partnership that had guided Coron through its darkest hours. Falon, her youthful exuberance tempered by the gravity of the occasion, marched proudly with the dwarf contingent, their axes gleaming in the sunlight. Elara and Finn, their wise eyes reflecting centuries of accumulated wisdom, followed closely, their presence a reassuring anchor. Behind them, a sea of Coronians marched, their faces a mixture of hope, determination, and a quiet joy. They carried banners depicting symbols of their resilience, their creativity, their dreams for a brighter future. Their songs of hope resonated through the ancient city, a chorus of voices united in purpose and vision.

The route to the grand plaza, where the coronation was to be held, was lined with onlookers. Their faces, once etched with worry and despair, were now alive with a sense of anticipation. They cheered, their voices a thunderous wave of support, washing over Gerald and the procession as they walked. Children tossed flower petals, showering the procession in a cascade of color, their small gestures adding to the jubilant atmosphere. The air was filled with a cacophony of sounds – the rhythmic beat of drums, the joyful cries of the people, the melodious strains of Coron's traditional instruments.

The grand plaza itself had been transformed. The devastation of Aldar's siege on Coron was barely perceptible beneath the vibrant tapestry of life and celebration. The shattered remnants of buildings were hidden behind colorful fabrics, and the scarred earth was adorned with wildflowers and blossoming trees, representing the promise of new growth. A magnificent throne, crafted from polished oak and adorned with precious stones, stood center stage. It was a symbol of Coron's resilience, and to their determination to rebuild and reclaim their destiny.

As Gerald ascended the steps leading to the Grand plaza, a hush fell over the crowd. The weight of expectation was heavy, yet he carried himself with a quiet confidence. He wasn't royalty in the traditional sense, but he was their storyteller, their Bridgebinder from another world. He had earned their trust not through conquest or intimidation but through compassion, empathy, and a shared vision.

Anya stepped forward, her voice ringing clear and strong. She addressed the gathered crowds, recounting the tumultuous journey they had undertaken, the struggles they had faced, and the spirit that had brought them to this momentous occasion. She spoke of Gerald's arrival, a stranger who had become an integral part of Coron, a man whose wisdom and their newfound courage had helped guide them toward salvation. She spoke of his efforts in restoring the city's infrastructure, ensuring the safety of the citizens, and uniting the people under a banner of hope and resilience.

The assembled crowd listened raptly, their attention captivated by Anya's words. Her tribute to Gerald was not merely a recital of facts; it was a narrative woven with emotion, the profound impact Gerald had on the lives of the Coronians. It was a tale of transformation, of hope found in the face of adversity, a tribute to the man who had stepped into their world and become their guiding light. Then, in a voice clear and resonant, she awarded Gerald the highest honor Coron had to give. His name would be written into the history of Coron, as a chosen figure, whose leadership had been forged in the crucible of crisis. The crowd erupted in thunderous applause, their voices a wave of support and affirmation.

It was a simple yet deeply moving event that reflected the essence of the Coronian spirit. There were no elaborate rituals or arcane incantations. Instead, Gerald spoke of unity, of collaboration, of shared responsibility, of building a Coron where every citizen had a voice, a purpose, and a stake in the future. His words, though not imbued with magic in the traditional sense, held a profound power; a power forged from truth, empathy and hope.

He looked upon the sea of faces before him – the artisans, the farmers, the soldiers, the children – and he saw their hope reflected in his own eyes.

The celebration continued long into the night. Music filled the air, the rhythmic beat of drums mingling with the melodies of flutes and stringed instruments. Dancing illuminated the plaza, bodies moving to the rhythm of shared joy and renewed hope. Food was shared, laughter echoed, and the people of Coron celebrated their newfound unity and their belief in a brighter future. The coronation was not merely an event; it was a turning point, a symbolic rebirth of a kingdom and the belief in its people's collective strength. Gerald, once a stranger, had become a symbol of this Kingdom. The new era had begun, not with the clash of steel, but with the gentle, persistent beat of hope.

The following years witnessed a remarkable transformation in Coron. The scars of war, though still visible in the weathered stones of the city, were slowly fading beneath a vibrant layer of renewal. The peace, won and fiercely guarded, allowed the kingdom to breathe, to heal, to rebuild itself from the ashes of conflict. Gerald, no longer just a stranger but a deeply respected leader, guided the process with a quiet determination, his decisions tempered by wisdom and empathy.

The kingdom's cultural richness blossomed during this period. Musicians, artists, and writers found renewed inspiration in the peace and prosperity that enveloped Coron. New festivals and celebrations emerged, reflecting the kingdom's newfound unity and optimism. The arts flourished, producing a wave of creativity that transcended the boundaries of language and culture.

Even the Sanctuary of Lost Souls experienced a renaissance. Elara and Finn, with Gerald's support, oversaw a major expansion of the Sanctuary, transforming it into a center of learning and healing. Scholars from across the land came to study the Sanctuary's ancient texts and unlock the secrets of its magical properties. The Sanctuary's resources were utilized to provide medical care and support to those in need, reinforcing its role as a beacon of hope and healing. The transformation of Coron was not without its challenges.

The newfound peace in Coron didn't just foster internal growth; it also extended its tendrils outwards, the possibility of reaching other kingdoms and realms. The initial hesitancy from neighboring lands, born from years of isolation, gradually dissipated. News of Coron's remarkable transformation, its emphasis on collaborative governance, and its blossoming cultural scene – spread like wildfire, captivating the imaginations of far off rulers and commoners alike. Embassies began to arrive, bearing gifts and proposals for trade and alliance.

One of the first to arrive was an envoy from the sun-drenched kingdom of Solara, a land renowned for its vibrant arts and exquisite craftsmanship. Their emissaries, adorned in shimmering silks and adorned with intricate jewelry, brought with them not only opulent gifts but also a troupe of musicians and dancers. Their music, a mesmerizing blend of strings and wind instruments, filled the grand plaza with its enchanting melody, while their graceful dances, inspired by the movements of the sun and the stars, captivated the Coronians. In return, Coron showcased its own unique cultural treasures: the storytelling tradition, the intricate weaving techniques of the dwarves, and the powerful, emotive songs of its bards. This cultural exchange was a beacon of hope, a symbol of the interconnectedness of worlds, demonstrating that even after the devastation of war, the spirit of collaboration and mutual understanding could prevail.

The Solarian artisans, in particular, were impressed by the ingenuity of the Coronians. They collaborated on a series of projects, combining Solara's expertise in glassblowing with the dwarves' mastery of metalwork. The resulting creations, breathtakingly beautiful and intricately designed, were displayed in a joint exhibition, attracting visitors from across the land. The collaboration not only produced stunning works of art but also fostered a deep bond of friendship and mutual respect between the two cultures.

Another significant connection was established with the kingdom of Aerilon, a land known for its mastery of aerial navigation and its advanced understanding of magic. The Aerilonians, renowned for their graceful airships and their expertise in celestial navigation, shared their knowledge of advanced weather patterns and star charting with the Coronians. This partnership proved invaluable, aiding Coron in the development of more efficient agricultural practices and enhanced navigation for its burgeoning trade routes. In return, Coron offered the Aerilonians access to its rich mineral resources, essential for the construction and maintenance of their airships. The exchange also involved a sharing of knowledge and techniques in healing magic, with both kingdoms contributing unique methods and understanding to the advancement of medical practices.

The cultural exchange was not limited to tangible goods and technical knowledge; it also encompassed philosophical ideals and artistic expressions. Philosophers from the kingdom of Veritas, renowned for its focus on logic and reason, engaged in lively debates with Coronian scholars, stimulating new avenues of intellectual inquiry. Their discussions, though sometimes spirited, fostered a greater understanding of different perspectives and a richer appreciation of the diverse ways in which knowledge could be pursued. Meanwhile, Coronian artists and musicians travelled to Veritas, exposing its inhabitants to a new range of emotions and expressive styles, adding fresh perspectives to their own artistic traditions.

The exchange with the kingdom of Sylva, a land heavily forested and steeped in ancient magical lore, resulted in remarkable breakthroughs in environmental stewardship. The Sylvans, masters of symbiotic living with nature, shared their knowledge of sustainable forestry and herbal remedies with the Coronians. This knowledge, invaluable in healing the land scarred by war, was embraced by the Coronians, creating a collaborative effort towards environmental restoration. In return, Coron's engineers, inspired by the Sylvans' ingenious use of natural materials, developed innovative designs for ecofriendly buildings and infrastructure, further strengthening the mutual respect and collaboration between the kingdoms. This collaboration proved to be a critical turning point, showcasing the potential of collaborative environmentalism in a world grappling with the growing impact of climate change.

The Coronians, once isolated and wary of outsiders, now welcomed ideas and perspectives, expanding their horizons and enriching their own cultural fabric.

The influx of new ideas, customs, and technologies from other kingdoms brought about a wave of innovation across Coron. New architectural styles, inspired by the elegant designs of Solara and the natural integration of Sylva, blended seamlessly with Coron's traditional aesthetic. New agricultural practices, based on the knowledge shared by Aerilon and Sylva, increased food production and ensured greater food security. The introduction of new artistic styles and musical forms added depth and vibrancy to Coron's cultural life. The exchange extended even to the realm of governance, with Coron adapting and enhancing its own systems based on the experiences and insights of other kingdoms.

The scars of war remained, engraved into the landscape and the memories of its inhabitants, but they served as a constant reminder of the peace that had been achieved. Gerald dedicated his time to mentoring the young leaders who were stepping into positions of power, sharing his insights and guiding them towards a future of lasting peace and prosperity. His home, a modest cottage nestled amongst the whispering willows near the Sanctuary, became a place of pilgrimage for those seeking counsel and inspiration.

The tales of his journey, his unlikely arrival, and his crucial role in defeating Aldar were scribed into epic poems and ballads, sung by bards in taverns and sung by children in their homes.

One ballad, titled "The Bridgebinder of Worlds," described Gerald's transition from a solitary writer grappling with his own inner demons to a courageous leader who helped unify a divided kingdom. The ballad became a staple at every Coronian celebration, reinforcing the kingdom's dedication to unity and collaboration.

The legacy of Gerald's actions help to establish the Royal Academy of Coron, fueled by his vision, attracted scholars from across the realms. Researchers embarked upon projects focusing on the unique magical properties of Coron, the history of its diverse cultures, and innovative approaches to technology. The Academy, a hub for intellectual curiosity and collaboration, thrived under the guidance of scholars inspired by Gerald's firm belief in the power of knowledge.

Even after his return to his own world, his presence continued to shape the destiny of Coron. The annual Bridgebinder Day became a vibrant celebration of life, unity, and the enduring power of hope. Parades filled the streets, bards sang his songs, and children reenacted scenes from his life, ensuring that his values and ideals remained at the heart of Coronian society.

15

Epilogue

The Gerald who had first stumbled through the shimmering portal into Coron was a writer, lost in the labyrinth of his own imagination, haunted by self-doubt and the looming deadline of a book that refused to write itself. He was a man adrift, clinging to the familiar comforts of solitude, oblivious to the adventure that lay just beyond his doorstep. The man who had been lost was now the man who had found his purpose.

His journey to Coron had been a brutal education. He had learned that courage wasn't the absence of fear, but the ability to act in spite of it. He had fought alongside beings whose existence once dismissed as fantasy – elves, dwarves, winged creatures of breathtaking beauty, and warriors whose strength and determination inspired awe. He learned their languages, their customs, their hopes and fears. Gerald laughed with them, cried with them, and felt their pain as deeply as his own.

Gerald's transformation extended far beyond the physical restraint. He discovered a wellspring of creativity fueled not by isolation, but by collaboration.

His understanding of storytelling had also undergone a profound metamorphosis. It seemed so insignificant now, a pale imitation of the epic saga unfolding around him. His journey to Coron through a magical portal had given him a fantastic adventure.

He also knew that his time in Coron had been more than just an adventure, more than just a tale. It was a transformation, a rebirth to the power of unexpected journeys. It was a story that would continue to unfold, not just in the annals of Coron, but within himself. A story he would always carry.

Sometimes, he would wake with the scent of pine and damp earth filling his nostrils, the image of Elara's determined face, or Finn's quiet strength and Falon's smile. These weren't mere dreams; they felt like visits, fleeting glimpses across the chasm that separated our worlds.

It was no longer an escape from reality, but a reflection of it, a means of exploring the complex interplay of power, magic, and morality, both within the confines of Coron and the larger tapestry of the interconnected realms.

The book he had initially struggled to write, the one that had seemed so insignificant before his journey, now felt different. It was no longer a mere collection of words on paper but a vessel, a conduit for his experiences.

Gerald began to research mythology, folklore, and ancient texts, searching for clues, for parallels, for answers. Looking for echoes of Coron in the myths and legends of different cultures, tales of travelers crossing between worlds, of heroes battling against formidable foes, of the delicate balance between worlds constantly under threat.

Gerald had truly become a Bridgebinder between worlds, a storyteller of far reaching journeys filled with adventure. The writing, now, flowed effortlessly, born of this deep understanding. The quiet hum of his typewriter became a rhythmic counterpoint of collaborated thoughts. The scent of old paper and ink, once a familiar comfort, now carried the faint, lingering aroma of pine needles and damp earth – the phantom scent of Coron. It was a fragrance that clung to his memory, a tangible reminder of a journey that had irrevocably altered his writing and storytelling.

Gerald found himself drawn to the complexity of characters who, like his companions of Coron, were faced with seemingly insurmountable odds. Their struggles, their triumphs, their vulnerabilities. Gerald's books were filled with tales of adventure, quiet courage, unwavering loyalty, fierce determination and mystical wonders. Gerald wondered if he would ever see that wonderous shimmering light which carried him to Coron and back. Only time will tell.